The Special Powers Act
Northern Ireland

Under the Act the authorities are empowered to:

(1) Arrest without warrant;
(2) Imprison without charge or trial and deny recourse to *habeus corpus* or a court of law;
(3) Enter and search homes without warrant, and with force, at any hours of day or night;
(4) Declare a curfew and prohibit meetings, assemblies (including fairs and markets) and processions;
(5) Permit punishment by flogging;
(6) Deny claim to a trial by jury;
• (7) Arrest persons it is desired to examine as witnesses, forcibly detain them and compel them to answer questions, under penalties, even if answers may incriminate them. Such a person is guilty of an offence if he refuses to be sworn or answer a question;
(8) Do any act involving interference with the rights or private property;
(9) Prevent access of relatives or legal advisers to a person imprisoned without trial;
(10) Prohibit the holding of an inquest after a prisoner's death;
(11) Arrest a person who "by word of mouth" spreads false reports or makes false statements;
(12) Prohibit the circulation of any newspaper;
(13) Prohibit the possession of any film or gramophone record;
(14) Arrest a person who does anything "calculated to be prejudicial to the preservation of peace or maintenance of order in Northern Ireland and not specifically provided for in the regulations."

Many thanks to everyone who read the text for their very helpful comments and suggestions.

Aly Renwick is a Scottish ex-soldier who spent eight years in the British army. Finally managing to buy himself out in 1968, he moved to London and joined the Vietnam Solidarity Campaign whose demonstrations he had taken part in while still a soldier. When the North of Ireland erupted in 1969 and British troops were sent onto the streets, he helped organise the Irish Civil Rights Solidarity Campaign and the Anti-Internment League. In 1974 he was a founder member of the Troops Out Movement and was one of their national organisers for several years. In 1978 he helped set up Information on Ireland and edited their first publication *British Soldiers Speak Out On Ireland*.

'It may be of interest to recall that when the regular army was first raised in the seventeenth century, "Suppression of the Irish" was coupled with "Defence of the Protestant Religion" as one of the two main reasons for its existence.'

Brigadier Frank Kitson
(*Low Intensity Operations*, 1971)

Guns at the ready. British troops face the Bogside rioters across a barbed-wire barricade

The author at Burford church in the summer of 1989. The memorial tablet was presented by members of the Workers' Educational Association and unveiled by Tony Benn in 1979. Below: From a postcard produced by the Friends of Burford Church.

This book is dedicated to the memory of the Levellers who refused to fight in Cromwell's army in Ireland in 1649, and especially to the memory of the three who were shot by a firing squad in Burford churchyard, then buried in unmarked graves.

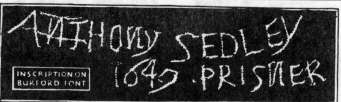

ANTHONY SEDLEY 1649 . PRISNER

INSCRIPTION ON
BURFORD FONT

Sunday 13 May 1649 : Many of Oliver Cromwell's soldiers, weary of his Tyranny, being order'd to fight against the Irish, refused. A party of them, trapped by Oliver at Burford, were on this & the next three nights prison'd in the Church, when Anthony Sedley wrote his name on the lead of the Font. Three of the 'Levellers' were shot in the Churchyard, while Sedley & the others watched from the roof.

From an original rubbing by B. C. Boulter

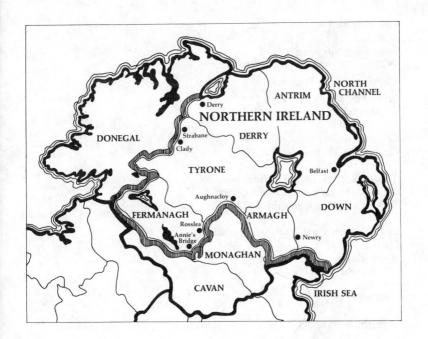

First published in 1989
A Barbed Wire book
From Information on Ireland
PO Box 958, London W14 OJF

Copyright © Aly Renwick 1989

Printed by The Russell Press Ltd.,
Gamble Street, Nottingham NG7 4ET

Cover Graphic: from *Love Triangle*,
Georgy and Vladimir Stenberg 1927

Thanks to P. Michael O'Sullivan for
use of photographs from *Patriot Graves*,
Follett Publishing Company, 1972

British Library Cataloguing in Publication
Data
Renwick, Aly
    Last night another soldier
    I. Title
    823'.914 [F]

ISBN 0–9512839–1–X

Trade distribution by
Turnaround Distribution, 27 Horsell Road,
London N5 IXL, tel. 01-609 7836
USA distribution by Connolly Books,
PO Box 24744, Detroit,
Michigan 48224, USA

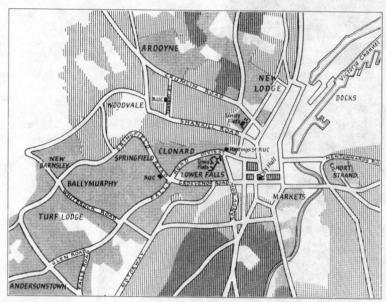

Belfast

Unionist/Loyalist areas
Nationalist/Republican areas
Mixed areas

Oliver's Army is here to stay,

Oliver's Army are on their way,

And I would rather be anywhere else than here today…

ELVIS COSTELLO

Part One

1963
Que sera, sera

Oh the time will come up
When the winds will stop
And the breeze will cease to be breathin'
Like the stillness in the wind
'Fore the hurricane begins
The hour when the ship comes in.

Bob Dylan

'Who are we?' 'We arra people!' Groups of chanting youths strutted through the grim streets, pushing through the crowd, all moving in the same direction. In the distance the floodlights glaring with a bright fluorescent intensity lit up the dull November evening. Ibrox like a neoned Mecca beckoned the faithful.

The massive current used to charge the lights seemed to transfer its energy to the streets and to the crowd itself as they hurried along to assemble for the match. For this was the big one, sometimes described as the greatest football match on earth. But Rangers versus Celtic is more than just a game, it is an annual war, using eleven selected warriors from each side to do battle for the cause.

The roots of the conflict go back to the roots of Glasgow itself, to the eighteen hundreds when a giant steelopolis emerged where once a sleepy little town lay at the mouth of the Clyde. To feed the needs of the ever-growing wheels of industrialisation, a steady stream of people poured in till the new-made city bulged at every corner. From the lowlands they came, lured by the false Klondyke of prosperity that industry promised; from the north came clanspeople dispossessed because sheep and deer had proved more profitable; and from Ireland they came, across the bitter sea, to escape repressive laws and starvation. Welded together by the raging heat of the furnaces, these sections of Glasgow's emerging proletariat still retained their separate histories, cultures and religions.

Nineteen-sixty-three had been a relatively stable year in Britain, but two years previously a national disaster had struck Scotland. The old enemy, England, at Wembley Stadium, had annihilated the pride of Scottish football nine goals to three. Frank Haffey of Celtic had been the unfortunate goalie who had picked the ball out of his own net so many times, and he knew from bitter experience that the Rangers fans would soon remind him of the debacle.

In some of the approach roads to the stadium the crowds were mixed. Even the colours seemed to clash as the supporters, in their scarves of red, white and blue, and green and white, hurried along on opposite sides of the street. Police were numerous, most on horseback carrying long-handled riot-batons, especially where the crowds diverged heading for their respective entrance gates.

Led by their cousin Jack, Sorcha and her brother Seán followed the green tide flowing to fill the Celtic end. As they joined the queue for the terracing Sorcha noticed the various vendors. Besides match programmes, collections were being made for various Catholic charities and 'Ireland one Island one Nation' songsheets were being sold. At the Rangers end the 'Protestant Ulster' paper was on sale, while another seller was making a killing with little union jacks on sticks.

Jack paid for the three of them and they pushed their way through the creaking turnstile and up the steep steps. They found themselves hustled into position down the terraces, closer to the Rangers fans than Jack had wanted. Although he felt uneasy it was pointless trying to push through to a more distant position, since they would only have lost each other in the tightly packed crowd.

The atmosphere created by the eighty thousand-strong crowd and the lights so bright glaring down onto the lush green pitch was both exhilarating and unnerving. The supporters were limbering up for the verbal battle: at the back of the terracing at the Rangers end a large contingent fronted by a Red Hand emblem were giving voice to their version of 'Derry's Walls':

> Then fight and no surrender,
> But come when duty calls,
> With heart and hand and Ralphy Brand,
> We'll guard old Derry's walls.

At the Celtic end tricolour flags were waving and 'Roddy McCorley goes to die on the bridge of Toome today' was starting to blot out the sound of the rival singing from across the way.

Rangers and Celtic were both formed in the latter half of the eighteen hundreds. Football flowered as a working class sport but increasingly came under the guidance and control of establishment influences. The sport was to retain its roots in the new proletariat of the cities, and every Saturday they could safely purge themselves of their frustrations at the match. Competition and rivalry between working people was promoted, while a successful club could be a money-making business in its own right.

Celtic emerged from Glasgow's growing Irish community, adopted green and white as its colours and flew the Irish tricolour over its ground, Parkhead. Rangers was formed by an association of Protestant youth clubs, had royal blue with red and white as its colours, and flew the union jack over Ibrox.

Celtic, the visitors, were first out and the sudden roar as the players emerged shook Sorcha to the core. The boos and jeers of the Rangers fans changed to an ecstatic cheer as their players came running out and started limbering up. An even louder roar rent the air as the referee blew his whistle and the match got underway.

The first half went disastrously for Celtic although for more than twenty minutes they had held their own. Then 'Slim Jim' Baxter, Rangers' left half, received a ball from defence directly to his feet. He moved effortlessly between two Celtic players, looked up and saw a flash of royal blue from Ralph Brand's back as he went on a forward run. Baxter stopped dead, sidestepped a lunge from a Celtic player and hit a thirty-yard pass over the heads of the remaining defenders into Brand's path. Just onside, Brand bursting through caught Haffey in two minds and cracked a low left foot drive into the corner of the net. Flushed with success the Rangers fans began to goad the Celtic goalie. The shout went up, 'What's the time?' and forty thousand throats roared the reply, 'Nine past Haffey.' Ten minutes later came Rangers' second goal; Wilson, Brand and Baxter weaved an intricate pattern up the left wing which finished with a far post cross. A demoralized Haffey moving too late missed the ball, leaving Rangers' centre forward Millar the simple task of nodding it over the line.

If the first half had belonged to Rangers then the second half was Celtic's. They launched wave after wave of attacks spearheaded in the main by John Hughes up the left wing. Known to the fans as 'Yogi', Hughes was over six feet tall and shuffled around the pitch like the bear he was named after. He was an enigma to the fans, missing open goals but scoring from the corner flag, sometimes dribbling through the entire opposition defence and at others falling over the ball when all on his own. But 'Yogi' was especially loved by the Celtic fans because he always seemed able to turn it on against the Rangers.

Twenty minutes remained, with the Celtic fans chanting 'feed the bear – feed the bear', when Hughes took off on a forward run, then cut inside and let loose a drive. The ball looked like it would go just over the cross bar of the Rangers goal but dipped at the last moment and suddenly was nestling in the back of the net. The equalizer came ten minutes later, when Chalmers ran onto a through ball and cut back a cross from the bye-line. Hughes running across the Rangers penalty area out-jumped the opposing centre-half, met the ball on his forehead and sent it looping over the outstretched arms of the Rangers goalie into the back of the net.

Celtic's tails were up, and victory was in sight with the cheers of the crowd reaching a crescendo, when with minutes to go came the match's most dramatic moment. Hughes had set off on another mazy run, beating two Rangers defenders in the process, and was moving into the penalty box when a tackle from behind floored him. The referee blew his whistle and pointed to the penalty spot. There was immediate chaos with Rangers players and fans protesting and Celtic players and fans ecstatic. The referee, despite the Rangers appeals, held his ground and insisted that the penalty be taken. The Celtic fans were quiet for an instant then chanted out their love for Hughes: 'Why do we call him Yogi?' Forty thousand throats roared out the reply, 'Cause he's smarter than the average Ranger.' Murdoch, Celtic's right half, took the penalty in text-book style, sending the ball into the left-hand corner of the Rangers goal.

Only seconds to go and Celtic were in front, then the trouble started. Suddenly fighting broke out at the areas where the fans met, and bottles and cans started to fly. Being fairly close to the rival fans, Jack, Sorcha and Seán were in an area that became a target for the Rangers throwers. It was frightening to see bottle after bottle come lazily through the air to shatter noisily on the concrete terracing. People began to panic and run in whatever direction they thought led to cover. Jack, Sorcha and Seán were suddenly engulfed in a larger group of fans shouting and pushing their way to safety. Sorcha tried desperately to keep in sight of Jack and Seán but in doing so lost her footing and crashed headlong over a terrace step. She scrambled quickly to her feet and looked around wildly but could see no sign of her cousin or brother. At the front of the terracing the fans were by now well mixed as both Rangers and Celtic supporters jostled around to escape the barrage of missiles from the back. Some fans had pushed over the barriers onto the pitch itself.

'Are you okay hen?'

Sorcha heard the voice behind and turning quickly found herself face to face with a youth about her own age.

'There's blood on your arm,' he said, pointing to her left wrist. Sorcha glanced down and saw the cut that a piece of broken glass had made when she fell; in the tension of the situation she had not felt or noticed the injury herself. She grabbed a hanky from her pocket and held it tightly over the cut to stop the flow of blood.

Sorcha glanced at the youth again and this time noticed the

red, white and blue scarf around his neck. 'I'll be all right, it's only a scratch,' she said, looking around again for Jack and Seán.

'We should get out of here,' the youth replied, and to emphasise his words another bottle smashed to fragments at their feet. They hurriedly followed others pushing their way towards the distant exits.

The match was over. After the police had cleared the pitch of spectators, the referee restarted the game then almost at once blew his whistle for full time. The crowds going out were even more compressed than they had been coming in. Sorcha seemed to be almost lifted up and carried along down the back of the terraces, compacted till she could hardly breathe, then bursting through the exit gates and into the street beyond. Once outside Sorcha glanced around again, up and down the street and around the milling crowd.

'Who did you come with?' the youth asked.

Sorcha turned round. 'My brother and my cousin,' she answered, then looking into his eyes added, 'We came to support Celtic,' wondering what reaction her words would have.

'We're not all perfect,' the youth said grinning. 'My name is Billy, Billy Johnstone. You don't sound as if you're from Glasgow?'

Before she could answer Sorcha heard a shout from the crowd and her brother and cousin came running towards her.

'I thought we'd lost you,' Jack exclaimed, as he arrived closely followed by Seán, relief written all over their faces.

Sorcha grinned. 'Oh, I was all right. I found my way out okay – with a little help,' she added, indicating Billy.

She was about to continue but her brother Seán, who had glanced at Billy and his Rangers colours, cut in. 'Why do the idiots have to cause trouble? Most of us on both sides just want to watch the match in peace,' he said, shaking his head. They all nodded their heads in agreement. There was silence for a minute and Sorcha glanced at the bustle around them.

Billy started to tell them about his friend who had been at the match with him, at the front of the terracing just inside the

Rangers section, when bottles had rained down on them from the back. 'My mate got real panicky, so I told him – cool it son. Look, if your name is on the bottle then there's nothing you can do about it. But he gave me this look and said, "Yea, well, you forget my name's Willie Younger and I'm getting the hell out of here."

'You can laugh,' Billy continued, grinning at their smiling faces. 'But that really was his name and he shot off like greased lightning, jumped over the front barrier. The last I saw of him he was running up the pitch with a big policeman in close pursuit.'

Suddenly mounted police arrived two by two up the middle of the street and a loudhailer told the milling crowd to move on.

'We'd best be on our way,' said Jack, pointing up the road.

'I'm off thataway,' said Billy jerking his thumb the other way.

They all shouted goodbyes as they hurried off in opposite directions.

Later on that evening Seán accompanied Jack to his local to get a drink before closing time. Sorcha sat with her aunt and uncle watching the news on TV. The police were hot on the heels of the great train robbers.... the Americans were helping the South Vietnamese to get over the assassination of their President during a military coup earlier in the month... and the people of Kenya, led by Jomo Kenyatta, were preparing for their forthcoming independence ceremony. The news ended with a report of the disturbances at the Rangers versus Celtic match.

'Well, lass, you've seen for yourself that we have the same problems here as you have in Belfast.' Uncle Donald said, smiling at Sorcha as he switched off the telly. He had worked in the ship-yards for over forty years and been a shop steward for most of that time. Uncle Donald liked to tell of the times when as a young man he had taken part in the struggles of the Red Clydeside era. He especially recalled the huge procession that had followed the coffin of John McLean in 1921.

'I remember the times in Belfast when partition happened,' said Aunt Cathy, still staring at the now silent TV.

She turned to Sorcha. 'Your granda, he worked in the ship-yards, till the riots happened. All the Catholics were chased out, he never worked again for twenty years. It made him very bitter.'

Aunt Cathy's voice tailed off, then she looked directly at Sorcha again. 'You don't hear much about troubles nowadays, but things haven't changed you know. Anyway I'm glad I got out.'

Sorcha remembered her mother talking about her elder sister who had left home when the family had found it difficult to make ends meet. Cathy had gone to Glasgow when distant relatives had written saying that a few of the toffs in the big houses in the squares off the city centre were taking on servants. She was taken on as a maid. The hours were long, the work sheer drudgery and the pay poor. But at least she lived in with meals found, so she could send most of her small pay home where it provided a very welcome contribution.

Five years later she had met Donald. Cathy had only gone out occasionally, for little walks around the parks or about the streets window-shopping. One Saturday she had been strolling along, her mind on a letter from home with its bits and pieces of news, when the street had suddenly filled with a noisy demonstration against unemployment. Like many of the others in the street Cathy went to the pavement edge to watch. Besides chanting slogans against the government and for the right to work, the marchers occasionally tried to encourage those watching to join in the demonstration.

Cathy had found herself at the front of the crowd of onlookers when a group of passing marchers took up a chant of 'Come and join us!' The excitement of the flow of marchers with their bright banners, and the solemn but enthusiastic looks on their faces, kindled a spark within her. But still she would not have moved to join in had not one of the marchers looked directly into her eyes and paused, one arm outstretched, to create room for her. Cathy hesitated a second, then jumped into the gap to join the demonstration. Donald had been that marcher and to this day could not explain what impulse prompted him to beckon Cathy onto the march. 'Perhaps I recognised a kindred spirit,' he always said. But anyway that was how they had met and they married a year later.

Two days after the match, on the Friday morning, Sorcha and Seán packed and made ready to return to Belfast. They said their thanks and goodbyes to their aunt, uncle and cousin, then made off towards the station. It was cold and a damp fog filled the air. Glasgow to Sorcha seemed depressing. It was as if the Clyde, after decades of suffering pollution from the city, was now reaping its revenge by sending out the freezing fogs which blanketed the grimy streets. She thought of Belfast which in many ways resembled Glasgow, albeit on a smaller scale, but which seemed fresh and clear compared to this dark and damp city on the banks of the Clyde.

Later on they climbed aboard the ferry which set sail from Stranraer, and Seán settled in the lounge compartment to read the paperback he had bought for the journey. Sorcha climbed to the top deck. It was brighter away from the city and a fresh breeze blew her hair over her face. She watched as the green hills of Galloway faded into the distance. The squawking seagulls following in the ferry's wake were fighting over some refuse that had been thrown overboard. A young couple with a transistor radio came up on deck and sat facing each other on one of the seats. They were laughing and joking, pushing and shoving each other in a mock fight over a photograph the woman held. The man had to move quickly to catch the radio as it fell off the seat during their struggle. He turned up the volume as he replaced it and the sound of the seagulls was drowned out by last month's number one hit, the Beatles' 'She loves you'.

As she stood, one hand on the rail, Sorcha's thoughts turned to Belfast. In a couple of years she would be leaving school: what did the future hold in store? She knew getting a job might not be easy. Jack had told them about Rangers never signing Catholic players. Some people said similar discrimination happened when you tried to get work in Belfast. Seán had told her about the questions he'd been asked on job interviews. Name, address, followed by school, which in any other place might seem totally innocent. But in Belfast it enabled the questioner to establish the religion of the interviewee. As a result Seán was unable to secure a permanent job though he did manage to get casual work on building sites with his da from time to time.

The man on the radio was playing a request... 'Doris Day's big hit from 1956.' Sorcha silently mouthed the words which she'd sung with her friends as they'd played in the streets:

> When I was just a little girl,
> I asked my mother – what will I be?
> Will I be pretty – will I be rich?
> Here's what she said to me.
> Que sera, sera,
> Whatever will be, will be,
> The future's not ours to see.
> Que sera, sera.

Darkness had gradually descended, and Sorcha's eyes followed the lights in the distance which indicated a fishing boat passing by some distance away. Amid loud squawks, many of the gulls sped off towards it leaving only a few of the birds following the ferry. The radio was now playing the current number one hit, 'You'll never walk alone', by Gerry and the Pacemakers. The woman on the seat jumped up. She pulled the man to his feet and together they slowly danced. Suddenly the urgent voice of an announcer cut into the song: 'We are interrupting this programme with news of a shooting, in Dallas, Texas. It is thought that the President of the United States of America, John F. Kennedy, may have been hit by gunfire in this incident.'

Part Two

1966
The times they
are a-changin'

Far away in dear old Cyprus,

Or in Kenya's dusty land,

Where all bear the white man's burden

In many a strange land.

As we look across our shoulder

In West Belfast the school bell rings,

And we sigh for dear old England,

And the Captains and the Kings.

Brendan Behan (The Hostage)

'I'm sorry boys but there was nothing I could do. We've been told to lay off a few men and yous know the rules, last in, first out.'

Billy stood stunned. When he and the other apprentices had been called into the yard manager's office they had been expecting to get their first year's progress reports. There had been rumours of course, talk of less and less orders, and of the fact that other countries with modernised yards could build cheaper. The decline of the ship-building industry in Britain was just beginning to bite.

There was sympathy from the other workers. 'That's terrible son, better luck in the future, eh! Acht you'll soon get a job in yin o' them factories.' But underneath could be detected the fear and uncertainty that the layoffs had caused. Men who had served decades of toil, who had become used to the tough routine, now cast worried minds to the future as the first waves of what was to become a world-wide economic recession lapped on Scottish shores.

'Hey, yous there, hang on a minute! Do yous fancy a job with a future?' The ex-apprentices were walking slowly out of the yard gates for the last time, talking softly to themselves, when they heard the shout. Billy, coming into work that morning, had noticed a landrover pulling a caravan stop outside. He hadn't

West Belfast with Cave Hill in the distance

takęn any interest then, but now a headboard was placed on the roof of the caravan. 'The Professionals,' the slogan stated boldly, 'for a great life in the British Army.'

The man who had shouted stood on the steps of the caravan and beckoned urgently. 'Come on boys, it won't cost you anything to have a look.'

The ex-apprentices looked at one another then crossed the street and followed the recruiting sergeant into the caravan. The inside walls were covered with posters, each stressing a different aspect of army life. The sergeant stood by a table which was piled high with glossy recruitment pamphlets.

'Okay boys, I won't keep you long. Thanks for coming across. We heard a rumour there might be layoffs in the yards so we thought we'd come along and do yous a favour.'

The sergeant picked up a pamphlet. 'I bet you're all upset about losing your jobs,' he continued, and Billy and his mates nodded their heads.

The sergeant looked sympathetic. 'Look lads, if I were to tell you everything about the army you'd probably think I was giving yous a load of bull, but let me stress one or two things. First there's security: we've had an army for hundreds of years and we'll have one for hundreds of years to come. We don't have layoffs – once in, you're in for as long as you like. Then there's the fact that everything's found – food, lodgings – so your wages are yours to spend on what you want. You've got good companionship, boys of your own age, plenty of sport. But best of all in my book is the travel. You could go to the far east, Hong Kong or Singapore, Cyprus and exercises in the West Indies, Africa, Canada and Australia, to name but a few.'

Some of the ex-apprentices had started to fidget and look out of the open door. The sergeant pointed to the stack of pamphlets. 'Look, thanks for coming in lads, I won't detain you anymore, but I want you to promise me one thing – that you'll all take a copy of our brochure here and give serious consideration to doing a real job in the professionals.'

Billy, like the rest, took a copy and stuffed it under his arm.

Then muttering their thanks to the sergeant they all set off for home.

The woman stared at Billy.

'And how long have you been unemployed, mister...' she glanced down at the card, 'Johnstone?'

This was now a regular occurrence for Billy, visiting the local labour exchange. He tried to smile. 'About three months now I think,' he answered.

The woman didn't smile back, but frowned instead. 'I'm sure you don't want to remain a burden on the taxpayer. Can't you find a job to your liking?' she asked.

Billy hesitated. 'Well I – I haven't yet. I'm still looking but.'

The woman slowly counted out his dole money. 'Let's hope you find something soon, eh!' she said, as she handed the money over.

On his way out Billy noticed the poster on its own near the exit: 'The Professionals... Security... Adventure...Travel,' it read. Perhaps he should have a read of the brochure that the sergeant had given him outside the yard gates, he thought. There were other jobs he could have tried for but none he really fancied, so it wouldn't do any harm to have a look. Anyway he was fed up with his present predicament – surely the army couldn't be any worse.

When Billy got home he went straight to his room and rummaged around till he found the recruitment pamphlet. He lay back on his bed and settled down to read. The first page told him about the long history of the regiment, whose soldiers came mainly from Glasgow and the Clyde valley. It then described army life, what a new recruit could expect, and finished with colourful portrayals of various overseas postings. Downstairs Billy's mother had started to hoover the floor, and as usual she turned up the volume of the radio so she could still listen as she cleaned. Billy, stretched out on the bed, clicked his feet together to the fast tempo of the Eurovision song contest winner, Sandie Shaw's 'Puppet on a string'. He put down the brochure as his mind drifted from grey Glasgow to far-off exotic places.

As Sorcha walked home her thoughts were on the job interview she had just left. She had seen the advertisment for junior office workers for the new city centre supermarket and gone along in high hopes. But the man had asked the same old questions.

'Which area do you live in?' He looked at Sorcha keenly as she answered.

'I see, and what school did you go to?' he continued.

After that answer he wrote something on the paper in front of him, then looked up at Sorcha shaking his head. 'I'm afraid the office jobs are already taken, but we do require one or two shelf-fillers in the supermarket. The pay's not a lot and you'll have to work odd hours, but it's a start.'

Sorcha had bitten her lip to stop herself from demanding why the interviews were still going on if the office jobs were gone. She choked back the question and said she would take the job offered. As she went out, four others were still waiting to be interviewed and the man was calling out 'next'. She did need the job, she kept telling herself. She felt she had to be bringing some money home. She had thought she might become a secretary or something like that eventually and had just completed a typing course. It'll do for now till I can get a better job, she said to herself over and over again.

Sorcha passed the Hastings Street peelers' barracks and continued up Divis Street towards the Falls Road. As she went she glanced curiously along the streets to her right. At the far end red, white and blue bunting was beginning to appear strung up between the houses, and union jacks were hanging from some windows. In two weeks time it would be the fiftieth anniversary of the battle of the Somme, when Carson's Ulster Volunteer Force, recruited into the British army as the thirty-sixth division, had burst forward against the German lines. The men had previously been commemorating King William of Orange's victory at the battle of the Boyne two hundred and twenty-six years before.

Many had worn orange lilies and some wore their sashes as they charged shouting 'No surrender!' only to be cut down in their thousands by deadly machine-gun fire.

As Sorcha passed into the Falls Road some of the houses still had a few tattered green, white and orange ribbons hanging, reminding her of the commemoration held in her own community some two months ago. They had celebrated the fiftieth anniversary of the Easter Rising in Dublin, when the rebels had declared an Irish Republic and upheld the continuity of Irish revolt against British rule. The rising was quickly suppressed and the leaders had been taken out one by one and executed. Sorcha's granda had told her about James Connolly, the last to be shot, who had lived on the Falls for a short time long ago. She remembered the chair in the corner of her grandparents' house that granda hadn't allowed anyone to sit on. Connolly had been addressing a mass meeting of 'linen slaves', as he called the women mill workers, and he needed a platform to speak from. Granda's mother had rushed out with the chair for Connolly to stand on and that piece of furniture had been sacred ever since. Soon after that Connolly had moved back to Dublin and to his death in front of a British firing squad a few years later.

Many centuries before that a sandbank had formed where the Farset stream joined the Lagan river. This became a crossing point called 'Beal Feirste', the mouth of the ford of the sandbank. A few thatched huts of the ferry people were the only dwellings until the Anglo-Norman conquests eight hundred years ago. Then the invaders noted its strategic position and constructed a small castle on the spot as part of a chain of fortifications built across the province. The pacification of Ulster took centuries to consolidate, but then Belfast changed from a garrison against the native Irish into a frontier town through which poured land-hungry settlers from Scotland and England. Emerging through conquest and colonisation, Belfast remained the heel of Britain's continuing foothold in Ireland.

As Sorcha turned into Clonard Street she cast a furtive look over her shoulder. A local man had just died in hospital after being shot in this street from a passing car a few weeks ago. The previous year Terence O'Neill, prime minister of Northern Ireland, had invited his Southern Irish counterpart Seán Lemass to talks in Belfast. This meeting had held hints of reforms for nationalists in the North and for a new relationship between the two parts of Ireland. Unionists had mobilised in opposition, led by a fire-brand preacher and founder of the Free Presbyterian church called Ian Kyle Paisley. Tension had risen as street agitation and protest meetings were organised and Catholics became victims of random attacks.

Very few native Irish lived in Belfast until the great build-up of industrialisation similar to that which occurred in Glasgow. Industry needed labour, so native and settler, nationalist and unionist, Catholic and Protestant, were attracted to the city which like a magnet dragged towards it the people from the surrounding countryside. Sharp antagonism still existed between settler and native and the latter found themselves hemmed into ghetto areas, the largest of which stretched along the length of the Falls Road. The mill-owners built houses for these workers, often naming the streets after great British battles or other imperial exploits on foreign fields.

Sorcha lived in Clonard where the small red-bricked terraced houses formed thirteen short narrow streets, some named after the heyday of the British empire in India: Kashmir Road, Lucknow Street, Bombay Street, Benares Street, and Cawnpore, the street where Sorcha lived with her ma Maura, her da Seán and her brother, Seán junior. Each house had an outside toilet in a tiny backyard which led out to the maze of back alleys which connected it all.

'My name is Sergeant Davidson, and these two,' the man gestured behind him, 'are Corporals Rennie and Dix.'

The newest batch of recruits for the Regiment stood passively staring in the direction of the voice.

'We'll be in charge for the next six weeks, in which time we will endeavour to knock some sense into yous about how the army operates, and more importantly how yous will operate inside the army.'

Sergeant Davidson looked them over slowly. 'We're here to train you, but you must realise that we are a team. I'm the one who will carry the can for you lot, so my message to you is very simple: you play ball with me and I'll play ball with you. But just remember this – it's my fucking ball.'

The recruits giggled nervously as the sergeant continued. 'Corporal Dix will now show you the camp. I would advise you to get yourselves sorted out quickly and get to bed. Training starts in earnest tomorrow. I want you all up bright and early, ready to get going. Okay off you go.'

Later that night Billy, lying in a strange bed, found it difficult to get to sleep. It will take some time to get used to living in this large hut with so many other recruits, he thought. Uncertainty gripped his mind. Have I done the right thing signing on? What if I don't like it? But he banished these thoughts. I've committed myself and I'll give it a go were his last thoughts before he drifted off to sleep.

Crash! Bang! Billy and the rest of the recruits jerked awake as Duty Corporal Dix smashed the empty fire-bucket against the metal frame of the beds again and again.

'Wakey, wakey, rise and shine! Hands off cocks, hands on socks!' yelled the corporal as he paced round the room. 'I hope none of you dirty bastards have been wanking, you'll need all your energy today. Come on get up, I'll be back in five minutes and God help anyone who isn't up.'

The training routine was difficult at first and took some time to get used to. But then, to most of the recruits, who were a fairly even mix of city and country youths, the time started to pass more quickly. The aim of the training was to take the recruits, who signed on as individuals, and mould them into cogs in the army machine. In the early days the emphasis was on physical training with the instructors yelling orders and hurling insults in an attempt to produce soldiers who would obey orders without question.

'You're like a poacher's dog, son, all bones and bollocks!' was yelled into Billy's ear as he tried desperately to complete some press-ups on the beam during his first session in the gymnasium. But undoubtedly the worst part of training was on the square, as the recruits in their strange-feeling uniforms were drilled unmercifully round and round. It was here that Sergeant Davidson and his corporals came into their own, screaming and yelling as they harried the new soldiers into some semblance of co-ordination. Here too, abuse was the order of the day, especially for the awkward and slow-witted. When the recruit next to Billy turned the wrong way at a command, the sergeant was at his side in an instant.

'If you don't buck up, I'll stick my prick in your ear and fuck some sense into you!' he bellowed with his mouth inches from the unfortunate's head.

Meanwhile Corporal Rennie dealt with another misfit. 'And why did you leave your village sonny? Was there another idiot there already?'

Billy luckily mastered the drill techniques fairly quickly and so escaped most of the invective dished out to the slower members of the squad.

After a few weeks of basic training, some recruits indicated that they were considering packing up and going back to civilian life. The two corporals were the first to hear of this and immediately tore a strip off those concerned.

'What are you? Fucking namby pambies, wanting to run home to yer mammies?' they shouted, adding in a quieter voice that it would reflect badly on the training staff if recruits were lost.

One of the new soldiers persisted in his efforts to get out. Called Willie Monroe, he came from a small village in the hills near the source of the Clyde. He was awkward at drill, coming in for much abuse, and found difficulty coming to terms with the rigid routine and discipline. Sergeant Davidson's response, when he heard of Monroe's intentions, was to call a special parade inside one of the huts. Ordering the squad to stand at attention, the sergeant then told Monroe to join him at the front.

'We have a chap here who wants to leave this man's army,' snarled the sergeant, pointing to Monroe while glaring at the rest of the recruits. 'Are there any more mummy's boys who'd like to join him?... No? Good.'

Sergeant Davidson turned from the squad to face Monroe. 'I've been watching you since you came here and I've not been impressed. You're like a big girl, you even waggle your arse like one. I think we'll have to call you Marilyn. You're not a fucking queer are you?'

The sergeant turned to grin at the squad, and most of the recruits giggled back. Turning back to Monroe his voice softened. 'Look son I know it's hard, but keep at it, we can even make a man of you. You don't want to go home a failure do you? They'll all say you couldn't take it.'

The sergeant turned back to the squad. 'I told you at the start that we are a team. You all know that next weekend is your first leave – well, leave in the army is a privilege and has to be earned.' Sergeant Davidson indicated Monroe. 'If Marilyn here fucks off, then that reflects badly on the staff, but especially me.' The sergeant jerked his thumb into his chest. 'I won't take that lying down, so I propose a deal. Yous persuade him to stay in and give this man's life a chance, and you'll get your leave as promised. Fail, and it's cancelled, and I'll have yous out Saturday and Sunday square-bashing.'

The sergeant glowered at the assembled recruits and then at Monroe, before shouting 'Dismiss!'

'Now come here Marilyn dear.' Monroe heard the voices and looked around, scared.

'Don't run off, we just want a little chat, and afterwards as a special treat we'll let you give us a wank with your sexy little bum, you fucking nancy boy.' A group of recruits descended on Monroe and carried him off bodily. Later, the word went round that he had retracted his application for discharge and that the weekend leave was still on. Billy noticed that from then on

Monroe always appeared dispirited. Though he completed his training, he became the butt of abuse from the recruits as well as the training staff and Monroe continued to be called Marilyn from the day of the parade in the hut.

In the early part of training the recruits did not have much contact with the camp officers. Sergeant Davidson taught them the correct way to acknowledge an officer when you met one: a salute if in uniform, and an eyes left or right, while holding your arms rigidly into your sides, if in civilian clothes. They were also told to call an officer 'sir' at all times, but only to speak when spoken to.

After three weeks of training, the lieutenant who was nominally in charge of the squad began to inspect the recruits on morning parades. He would walk casually around the assembled men glancing at each in turn, sometimes touching a part of a man or his webbing with his swagger stick.

'Boot laces are twisted! Are these brasses really clean, sergeant? This fellow needs a haircut and I don't think he has washed properly.'

Sergeant Davidson, followed by a corporal, trotted behind snarling at anyone who attracted the officer's attention and handing out extra duties as a punishment.

One day Billy and another recruit were excused an extra drill parade in order to unload a few packing-cases into the officers mess. It was the first time Billy had been near the building which stood on its own, surrounded by lawns and flower beds, at the far end of the camp complex. The inside reminded Billy of the boardroom at the shipyards which he had once seen. The floor was highly polished and oil paintings of battle scenes hung on the walls amid gleaming wood-panelling. He was surprised to learn that twelve soldiers worked in the mess full time as valets, waiters and cleaners.

It was one of the busiest days Sorcha had known. People crowded through the supermarket all day and she was kept busy restocking shelves.

It was the official opening day of the new bridge over the Lagan. There had been controversy over the name: Paisley had wanted to call it Carson's Bridge. The authorities circumvented his scheme by naming the bridge after the Queen and inviting the royal lady herself to carry out the official opening.

On this the big day loyal crowds poured into Belfast's centre, many decked out in red, white and blue and clutching union jacks. At lunch in the city hall the Lord Mayor of Belfast told the Queen and the Duke of Edinburgh that there was no corner of the United Kingdom where the royal visitors would receive a more sincere or more loyal welcome than in Ulster.

Sorcha sang to herself as she made her way home that evening. Although she had not taken part in the celebrations herself, the loyal crowds had been happy and good-natured and she felt caught up in the atmosphere.

'Hey Sorcha, the peelers are at your house.'

She was nearing her street when the shout from an anxious neighbour brought her to a halt. When Sorcha asked why, the woman shrugged her shoulders, but added, 'There's two landrovers there too.'

Sorcha hurried round the corner into her street, and saw three policemen filing out of the door of her home. She hesitated as the peelers got into the front landrover, one adjusting the holstered revolver on his waist belt as he did so. The police vehicles roared off as she reached her front door and rushed inside.

Her da sat in his big armchair staring into the fire, and did not look up and greet her as normal. She heard a clattering of crockery as her ma prepared tea in the back-kitchen and hurried through.

'The peelers?' Sorcha gasped.

'It's all right love.' Her ma laid her hand on Sorcha's arm. 'You know your da works on that site in the centre, well someone threw a brick at the Queen's car as she passed by the day. It hit the car but didn't hurt anyone.'

Sorcha still looked puzzled. 'But daddy? Surely he didn't do it?' she asked.

'Not at all! Sure it was another lad who works there, but the peelers are going daft about it. They took the names and addresses of everyone and now they're paying visits.'

Sorcha knew her da to be a mild-mannered man who never got involved in politics, but his father had been a republican activist who had been imprisoned due to his involvement.

'The peelers kept bringing up your granda's name. Said your da must be following in his footsteps,' her ma said as they made ready to carry the tea through.

Sorcha looked at her da who still sat staring into the fire. She went over and put her hand on his shoulder. 'Don't worry daddy, it'll soon blow over,' she said, smiling down at him.

He looked up and gave her a weak smile, then the worried look crossed his face again. 'The peelers said the B-men were mad, they were guarding the route you see, they said I might get a visit from them.'

Sorcha's hand tightened on her father's shoulder as he spoke. 'They can't do anything to you daddy, you've done nothing,' she said comfortingly.

When Sorcha came home the next night she found her da sitting in his chair staring into the fire again. Her ma beckoned her into the back-kitchen.

'Your da got his cards the day, all our crowd on that site got it. He's on about going over the water again, he reckons he'll get work there, not get bothered like.'

During the summer Sorcha took to walking around the streets during her lunch breaks. One day she headed north enjoying the warm sunny weather. She was thinking of turning back when she passed a second-hand bookshop in the Antrim road. She glanced into the window at the rows of old books and noticed some paperback light romances like her ma often read. Sorcha glanced at her watch: it was really time to be getting back, but she pushed open the bookshop door and went inside. The shop was stacked with books of all sorts, laid out in bookcases around the walls and stacked on top of each other in rows up the middle. There did not seem to be anyone in attendance, although a bell had sounded as she entered. Sorcha looked at a stack of books, glanced at her watch again and was about to leave when a middle-aged man suddenly appeared from a side door. The man was thin-looking and limped on his left leg.

'Can I help?' he asked, with a trace of a foreign accent Sorcha could not identify. She told him about the books in the window saying they were for her ma. The man moved a bookcase to enable him to reach into the window and pull out the books.

'Sorry I was so long,' he said, handing them over.

'I need some help really,' he continued, as Sorcha rummaged through the books and picked out two.

'I was trying to type a letter, one-finger typing, it takes me ages,' the man said as Sorcha paid him for the books. She had been only half listening to what he'd been saying but her ears pricked up at the mention of typing. She forgot about hurrying back to work and offered to type his letter.

The man looked pleased and ushered her through the side door, down a short passage and into a side room cluttered with paperwork. Against the window stood a small table with an ancient typewriter on it. Sorcha took out his piece of paper and inserted a new sheet, and the man dictated his letter, which was about arranging to visit a house to look over a collection of books with a view to possibly purchasing them.

It took all of her concentration to remember her typing but the skill quickly came back. So after a hesitant start and having to ask the man to repeat the words a few times, she soon completed the letter. The man was delighted and, as he thanked her, Sorcha asked him if he'd been serious about taking on some help.

He hesitated. 'I would like to, I certainly need to, but I can't pay much.'

He went on to explain that he wanted to expand into the rare second-hand book market but found it difficult while running the shop. Sorcha told him where she worked, how much she was paid, and how she wanted to work at a job that at least had a bit of office work. The man seemed pleasantly surprised and said he would be willing to take her on at the shop as long as it was regarded as a trial period to start with.

'Let's see how it works out,' he said, promising to pay a bit more than she received at the supermarket. They shook hands on the deal.

When she hurried back to her shelf-filling Sorcha was told off for coming back late. She smiled sweetly and told them she was leaving the supermarket at the end of the week to start her new job on the Monday.

Later on, as she told her ma about her good luck, Sorcha bubbled over with enthusiasm. 'He didn't even ask me where I lived, or what school I went to, mammy. He wasn't interested, he wants me 'cause he thinks I'll be a help. I said I came from Clonard, West Belfast, off the Falls, just to see if it would make a difference. I might as well have said Timbuktu for all the interest he took in it.'

Billy lay sprawled on his bed. Only another week to go and training will be finished, he thought. It was more interesting now anyway, learning how to handle weapons and basic infantry manoeuvres. There had been a couple of exercises, digging fox-holes for defensive positions and laying ambushes. This had been exciting, especially the one at night when they'd been issued with blank rounds for their self-loading rifles, and with a giant banger called a thunderflash that went off with a massive boom.

Billy reflected on his life in the army so far. He felt vaguely uneasy about the routine he had slipped into, going through the motions of parades, drills and exercises with the others, then either lying on his bed reading comics or going to the NAAFI and drinking in his time off. Well at least the life was easy once you got into the routine, someone was always there to tell you what to do and it was a worthwhile job after all. What was it Sergeant

Davidson kept telling them? 'Every country needs an army and Britain has more reason than most to be proud of hers.'

Billy's thoughts then drifted back to his life before joining up. He remembered his work in the shipyard: what a shame to have lost out, he thought. What he would have liked best of all would have been to have stayed on and completed his apprenticeship. But fate had decided otherwise, well that's the way it goes, you just have to make the best of your lot. They say unemployment is rising, so soon others will be feeling the pinch. He thought of his mum and dad and the tenement block where they lived. He missed them, he missed the friendliness of the people, the good natured banter of his mates in the yards, going out on Friday nights, and the match on Saturday afternoons. He shook his head and glanced at his watch.

'Fancy a pint, Jimmy?' he called to another figure sprawled on the bed opposite. 'We'll just have time for a couple before they close the NAAFI.'

'We told you we'd make men of you. We kept our promise didn't we?'

The recruits were packed into the upstairs room of the Springbok pub which was just across the road from a back entrance to the barracks. It was one of Sergeant Davidson's favourite haunts and he was now addressing the assembly.

'... and now before we get down to the serious business of the regimental farewell bevvy, lads, Major Monteith, the adjutant, would like to say a few words.'

Some soldiers jumped to their feet as the major entered.

'Okay chaps, at ease; no need to rise, just a few words. I can't stop long, have a do on at the mess later. I just want to say that we are constantly pleased by the high standards reached by the recruits passing out from this establishment. Due credit must be given to the training staff,' the major indicated Sergeant Davidson.

'But we recognise that high standards can only be reached if we have first-class material in the first place. I've been looking at your reports and some of them are very good indeed – good show, keep up the good work. We live in testing times but just look at our history and you can see that Britain has survived as a great nation in a sometimes hostile world only by having armed forces that are second to none. It's chaps like you who have to keep up that tradition.

'I notice that most of you have got postings to the second battalion in Germany. Some may be disappointed by that, dreaming of more exotic places, what! Well in Germany you'll be taking part in the most important training that the present army does, facing a menace at least as big as any Britain has ever met before. Remember you are ambassadors as well as soldiers, remember you are soldiers not just of the British army but of this regiment as well. Carry that name and yourselves with pride. Right chaps keep up the good work, bye bye.'

Billy's recollections of the rest of the night were somewhat hazy as the now fully fledged soldiers embarked on an attempt to drink the Springbok dry. He did remember however that later on they persuaded Sergeant Davidson to sing a few of his stock of army songs. The last he sang was his favourite, which always went down well at such gatherings, called 'The Tattooed Lady':

> One night in gay Paree,
> I paid five francs to see
> A tattooed French lady,
> Tattoed from head to knee.
> On her jaw was a British man-o-war,
> And on her back was a Union Jack,
> So I paid three francs more,
> And on her tits were two full rigged sailing ships,
> And on her fanny was Al Jolson singing 'Mammy'.

As the weeks passed Sorcha began to enjoy her new work at the second-hand book shop. The man said to call him Victor and she learnt that he had come from Germany but had lived in Belfast for about twenty years. At the start, although she had to tend the shop when Victor was out on business, Sorcha's main task had been to bring the office into some semblance of order. Methodically she set about the paper work, gradually sorting it into categories and filing it in folders in the cabinet.

She was sitting in the office one day, struggling to balance the accounts with figures that never seemed to add up, when the shop bell rang. Victor was out so she happily left the papers and hurried through to the shop. A young man was peering at a shelf of books through his national health specs. He looked a bit like John Lennon, Sorcha thought, as she asked him if he needed any help.

'No,' he said, then hesitated. 'Well, perhaps... I'm a student at Queens, studying law.'

He looked familiar: Sorcha thought for a moment, then remembered. A few times she had been sitting at the shop desk and had looked up to notice the man peering at books in the window. He had always walked away when she had glanced at him, and this was the first time he had entered the shop.

'I don't think we have any law books,' Sorcha said.

His face went a bit red. 'No, no, I've plenty of those anyway. I wanted some light reading, the law books get a bit heavy at times.'

Sorcha motioned towards some shelves of novels in the far corner. She noticed he had a country accent and asked him where he came from.

'A wee place near Newry,' he replied.

Sorcha was pleasantly surprised as her family had originally come from that area. 'I have relations thereabouts,' she said, and told him their names and where they lived.

The man seemed delighted to recall that he had gone to school with a distant cousin of hers, and they continued to talk about the area which Sorcha knew fairly well through family visits. He told her his name was Frank McCarron and his father was a doctor in a village just outside Newry. They were still talking when Victor returned and went through to the back room carrying a box of books.

'Well, I mustn't keep you,' Sorcha said, indicating once again the shelves where the novels were.

He made no move in that direction. 'I, actually came in to see if you wanted to... if you would come out one night,' he stuttered, and his face went a bit red again.

Sorcha smiled. So that was it: he hadn't been interested in the books at all. Still, he had a nice face, she thought.

'What did you have in mind?' she asked.

'I've got two tickets for Friday night for Van the man,' he said excitedly, jerking his thumb to a leaflet in the window. Victor kept a space there where he would put up notices if requested, and Sorcha recalled the one advertising 'The Belfast Cowboy', as Rolling Stone magazine called Van Morrison who was coming home from America to give a concert. She agreed to meet a delighted Frank outside the venue.

Billy felt pleased with himself. From the porthole of the RAF jet he could see the vast expanse of sand dunes and gullies that made up the desert of Saudi Arabia. They had just completed a midway re-fuelling stop in Bahrain and were now proceeding on to Kenya. Billy was one of the lucky ones. Most of the soldiers from the training unit had gone to Germany, but five of the best recruits had been sent to make up the strength of the third battalion based at Lanark on the upper Clyde. Third batt was attached to the 'Strategic Reserve', an amalgamation of various units which made up a fighting arm, ready at a few minutes notice to travel to any trouble spot and 'sort out the aggro' as the sergeant put it.

Billy was proud he had been one of the five chosen. The rest of the unit was made up of old sweats, many of whom had taken part in some of the post-second world war campaigns that the British army had fought in. The soldiers were to take part in a six week training exercise to attune the unit to fighting techniques in jungle and scrubland terrain.

In Nairobi the men soon unloaded their equipment and set off for the transit camp which was only a short distance from the airport. Billy had found that some veterans adopted a rather patronising attitude towards him and the other new soldiers.

'Get some time in before you open your cakehole,' they would say if they felt a rookie had spoken to them out of turn. Billy however was not unduly put out by this because he had already made friends with some old sweats and felt he could learn a lot from their experience.

Later on the afternoon of their arrival, they were given a briefing by the unit commanding officer. They were told that the exercise area was many miles up-country near the town of Nyeri and would stretch from the lower foothills of Mount Kenya to the Aberdare mountain range. The soldiers were also told that the main inhabitants of the area were the Kikuyu tribe, who, although the soldiers would in the main find them friendly, should not be trusted and as little contact as possible should be maintained.

There was one soldier in the unit who excited Billy's curiosity because of the rumours circulating about him. His name was Neil McKinnon, and Billy first learned about him from another soldier when they were both engaged in trimming a hedge back at the barracks in Scotland. A group of officers had strolled by at a distance laughing and joking with each other.

'It's a pity McKinnon didn't sort out a few more of them,' said the soldier working beside Billy, jerking his thumb in the officers' direction.

Billy was mystified and asked the other soldier what he meant.

'Haven't you heard? Well it goes back to when we were in Aden, Neil was a corporal when we first went there and then something happened and he got busted. Anyway, we had this captain who was second-in-command and he was a right bastard – did everybody on parades, extras, extras and more bloody extras. In Aden he started sneaking up on the sentries. If he got near without being seen he'd do them for being half asleep, and even when he was challenged he'd say it wasn't done properly.'

The soldier smiled grimly at Billy. 'But McKinnon sorted him out. He was out on sentry duty one night and we heard this burst of firing. We all grabbed our guns and rushed outside. There wasn't any more shooting so we took a look, when we got to Neil's position there was this captain lying with a gut full of lead. Stone cold dead he was, Neil had emptied a full magazine from a sterling into him.'

'Jesus! Didn't he get into a lot of trouble?' asked Billy.

The other soldier smiled. 'Well, they tried to do him all right, they were going to court-martial him. But at the inquiry Neil just stuck to his story: that he'd seen a shadowy figure, that he'd challenged him twice and only fired when he received no reply, just like it said in the rules. They didn't believe him, but the only person who could have proved his story wrong was dead, so they gave up after a while. But they haven't forgotten, they still hate him. Neil's put in to buy himself out a few times and they always turn him down.'

They left the transit camp early next morning in a convoy of three-ton trucks which took the unit to their base camp area at the edge of the jungle-clad foothills of Mount Kenya. Under the eagle eye of the sergeant-major the men set to, putting up the tents that would provide their living quarters. After this task was completed the soldiers were allocated in twos a tent to sleep in. Billy was surprised and a little apprehensive when he found he would be sharing with Neil McKinnon.

For the first two weeks the exercise consisted of jungle warfare training in the areas surrounding the camp. The beauty of the countryside was impressive and the climate was much to the soldiers' liking too. It could get very cold at night and still be chilly in the early morning, but then the sun would slowly appear from behind Mount Kenya, warming up another day. From then on it was just like a hot summer's day back in Scotland. Billy could see the attraction for the white settlers who had come to this area when Kenya first became a colony and who still owned many of the farms they passed during training.

After a few months at her new job Sorcha arrived home one evening to find her ma crying and her da sitting by the fire in his best suit with a packed suitcase resting against his chair. Sorcha's ma saw the questioning look on her face and dried her eyes.

'The peelers came for your da again, took him into the Springfield Road barracks for a couple of hours. They asked him about the brick thrown at the queen again, kept on about your granda, him having been a IRA man and that.'

Sorcha's da looked up at her. 'They showed me to the B-men,' he said.

'There were some B-Specials there, said they wanted to see your da,' her ma explained.

'Said I was a troublemaker, needed to be taught a lesson,' her da cut in again.

Sorcha looked at them both and then at the suitcase. 'Where's daddy going?' she asked.

'He's been on about trying his luck at the building game across the water, sure you know yourself he hasn't been in work since they laid him off,' her ma replied.

Later that night Sorcha and her ma hugged and kissed her da, and the two Seáns solemnly shook hands, before her father picked up his case and made his way aboard the night ferry to Liverpool. After watching the boat leave the quay and vanish into the darkness the three made their way home in silence. Seán went off with some friends while Sorcha made a pot of tea and sat drinking it with her ma in front of the fire.

'I wouldn't have minded if your da had been involved in things, like your granda,' her ma said suddenly. 'God knows he tried to get your da involved, you know, but your da wasn't interested. It's hard enough trying just to live, he used to say. He was always a quiet man your da, that's what's so unfair. But as he himself said, once they've got your name on their list they won't leave you alone.'

Sorcha could see her mother was upset so she moved across to sit on the side of the armchair and put an arm around her ma's shoulders.

'You're a good girl,' her ma said, putting her hand on top of Sorcha's. 'Seán is like his daddy. I know he likes to get out for a good time, but he's a mild-mannered creature like your da.' She looked up into Sorcha's eyes. 'You're the one that's like your granda. I can't put my finger on it, but you remind me of him.' Her hand pressed tighter on Sorcha's. 'Pray God we'll never get the times we had in the past back again. I thought that was all finished.'

Later on that night as Sorcha made ready for bed she switched on the radio. They were playing Bob Dylan's hit from two years ago:

The line it is drawn – the curse it is cast,
The slow one now will later be fast,
As the present now will later be past,
The order is rapidly fadin',
And the first one now will later be last,
For the times they are a-changin'.

Sorcha switched off the radio and lay back in bed thinking of her da, things they had done, places they had visited, and she wondered how he would manage across the water on his own. Then a memory of her granda came into her mind. She remembered a sunny day, it seemed ages ago, she'd just been little and her granny and granda had taken her away from the hard streets and into the soft green countryside. They had slowly climbed a large hill overlooking the city, to a raised flat area at the top where they had sat looking out over Belfast. Her granda had then told her about the United Irishmen.

'The founders of our republicanism,' he had said, and told how a long time ago Tone, Russell, McCracken and a few others had, at this very spot, made their solemn pledge, 'never to desist in our efforts until we had subverted the authority of England over our country and asserted her independence.'

When the day's exercises were over there wasn't much for the soldiers to do. A beer tent had been set up and most of the men went there to spend the evening drinking and listening to the veterans talk about the various campaigns they'd been involved in. Billy was concerned because his tent mate Neil started disappearing almost every evening, only to reappear about midnight and settle down to go to sleep.

One night he was even later than usual and Billy was peering anxiously out of the tent flap trying to think where he might have got to, when Neil suddenly appeared out of the dark and pushed his way into the tent.

'Worried about me, eh?' he asked.

'Aye, I was, a wee bit. I wondered where you'd got to,' Billy replied.

Neil glanced at him. 'You know what wonder did, he stuck a feather up his arse and wondered if that made him a chicken.' Neil glanced at Billy again and saw the wounded look on his face. 'I didn't mean to be sharp, son, but there's too many loose tongues around. That's why I don't like people knowing my business.'

'I know how to keep my mouth closed,' Billy said fiercely.

Neil grinned, 'I'll tell you what, do you know how to play draughts?' he asked.

Billy looked surprised. 'Draughts? Yes I've played them. I could hold my own with my mates in the pub, but the old man could always beat me,' he replied.

'Good, good. Tomorrow evening we'll go for a wee walk and I'll show you where I get to. But remember mum's the word, we might get into trouble if anyone finds out.'

Billy was very curious but didn't ask any more questions. He lay back in the sleeping bag and wondered what the hell Neil's walk could have to do with draughts.

Luckily next evening neither Billy nor Neil were required for camp duties so after tea they set off. Neil led the way down to the stream where all the men washed in the morning, then casually strolled along the bank till a bend hid them from the camp. Neil then turned to Billy.

'Right, follow me as quick as you can,' he said.

They set off at a quick trot, continuing along the bank of the stream until it ran into a thicket-clad area bulging out from the main jungle of the foothills. They now took a path that led through the bush for about a mile. Suddenly the jungle fell away and they came to an expanse of open countryside. In front of them, next to another stream, were a few rows of rough timber-constructed huts. It was a little Kikuyu village. No adults were visible, but at the far end some children played football with a polythene bag filled with rags and tied with string.

Neil grinned at Billy and indicated with his hand. 'You wanted to know where I go at night, well here you are, our local village.'

Neil stopped talking when he saw the worried look on Billy's face. He frowned, then continued, 'I hope you don't believe that crap they give you, that you can't trust the natives. Listen, I've been all over with those fucken officers, they always give you the same patter no matter where we go. The reason's simple, they never know when they'll need us to put the boot in. That's why they give us the "wogs are all rubbish" patter, because if they didn't, and we got friendly, we might not fancy dishing out the aggro, if it came to that.'

Neil looked at Billy then started walking purposefully towards the huts, speaking over his shoulder as he did so. 'Anyway I'm telling you the people here are okay, so come on. You'll have to come 'cause you'd get lost if you tried to go back on your own.'

Billy following somewhat reluctantly behind was surprised when the children, who had just noticed their presence, ran with shrieks of delight towards them. Neil knelt down on one knee and drew a bar of chocolate from his pocket. He broke it into squares and gave one to each child, then jumped to his feet and gave a mighty kick to the rag ball which the youngsters then chased after. Neil then led the way to a larger hut set midway along a row and, pulling back the sacking covering the entrance, beckoned Billy to enter. The room seemed packed with Africans, some of whom smiled in the direction of Neil. In the far corner a large pot of water boiled over an open fire.

'Two glasses of tea,' Neil called out to the woman by the fire, indicating two with his fingers before he was engulfed by a group of Africans patting him on the back.

'We beat you this time, this time we win,' they said, dragging Neil off to a small table marked out in squares to form a draughts board, with bottle tops different ways up used for the counters. The woman brought two glasses of tea over and Neil paid her, then told Billy to get into the queue that was forming to play draughts. Neil played five games before he was beaten, to cries of delight, by an old African who continued at the table while Neil joined the back of the queue. When Billy's turn came he won twice before he was beaten. By now his initial inhibitions had been overcome and he was enjoying himself. He found the Africans' delight at entertaining new friends infectious. Their evident zest for life reminded him in a way of Friday nights back in the pubs of Glasgow, when people forgot their worries and went out to have a good time.

Later, on the way back to camp, Neil told Billy how he had seen the village one day during training and noted its position, then visited it that night for the first time. After chatting to a few Africans and finding that most spoke a smattering of English, he found out about the hut where the draughts were played, which he now called the 'local cafe'.

After the first two weeks, the unit started to travel around a lot to involve the men in exercises designed to test the various techniques they had learned. This made it difficult for Neil and Billy to visit the village very often, but they did so when they could. Once they halted for a period in Nyeri and Neil managed to do some shopping. On the next of their visits to the village he presented the children with a plastic football and gave the 'local cafe' a cardboard draughts board and plastic black and white counters.

During their fifth week in Kenya Neil pulled off a stroke that made him even more unpopular with the officers. The squaddies had been annoyed that although papers from Scotland were coming in with the mail they were all diverted to the officers and NCOs. So the ordinary soldiers didn't even know the football results, or receive any information about events or home news that might have interested them. A few months before, Neil had taken out a subscription with a local newsagent back in Lanark for the communist Morning Star paper. When he knew he was going on the exercise to Kenya, Neil had left money for a month's issues of the paper to be sent on by parcel post to the unit's forwarding address.

After he had received and read the papers Neil passed them on to the other soldiers. Most would normally have shied away from reading such a paper, but the lack of any news from home overcame this and soon Morning Stars were appearing all over the camp. The officers were outraged when this came to their notice and were not long in finding out who was responsible for the 'dirty deed'. But there wasn't much they could do about it except make sure there was an adequate supply of ordinary papers to dish out to the squaddies. Within a few days the men were showered with a regular supply of safe reading matter from the Fleet Street presses.

Billy had heard a sergeant describe McKinnon as 'that fucken commie', and he knew most of the officers and NCOs regarded Neil in a somewhat similar light. Many of the squaddies on the other hand said it was just a ploy he had adopted to help him to get out of the army.

Billy wasn't sure what to make of it. He had known a few of the men and some of the shop stewards in the shipyards had been communists. He had felt no antagonism towards them, indeed the yards of the Clyde had a history of workers' struggles in which communists and others of the left had played a prominent part.

But in the army? Surely that was different.

Since joining Billy had felt more and more distanced from his old life. Even the way he felt about things was changing. In the army all thinking and comment seemed to go in one direction. Perhaps it was the briefings given by the officers or the less subtle but more direct comments of the NCOs. Even the padre got in on the act. Billy remembered the church parade they had all attended before leaving for this exercise. The padre had prayed for an end to a current strike, hoped that the strikers would come to their senses, castigated the communists who were behind it, and made a plea for support for the good and stable influences in society which included the Tory party and the royal family.

When he got a chance, Billy asked Neil if he really was a communist or was he just putting it on to speed his discharge.

Neil grinned and shrugged his shoulders. 'I don't know, to tell you the truth. It started when I found it put their backs up. I got a few communist books and left them around where they would be seen. But reading them? I found them hard to understand, they seemed to be written by academics for other fucking academics to read.'

Neil scratched his head then looked at Billy again. 'I was talking to Karari the other night, he's the grey-haired old man who always beats me at draughts. Well, he told me about the war here before they got black rule. He said some of the fighting took place around here. The Africans were fighting our lot. We called them Mau-Mau, but Karari said they were called the Land Freedom Armies, there's a monument to them in Nyeri High Street. He said the British made this area a prohibited zone, and our aircraft bombed and shot anything that moved. Lots of blacks were slaughtered and lots put into barbed wire prison camps.'

Neil looked at Billy again, shaking his head. 'Anyway I'm determined to get out, I've got another application in to buy myself out. I've got high hopes this time. You know the new OC is a bit of a bible puncher? Well, I heard from a mate that when he did a room inspection he always looked at the squaddies' locker cards to see their details and what religion they are. When I knew he was to do his first inspection of us, I cut the red star from a Morning Star and glued it onto the space marked religion on my locker card. Mine was the last bed in the room and he'd gone round the rest looking at the cards and asking if the boys went to church regularly. He pushed past me to look at my card and there was dead silence, then he came and stood in front of me and his face went from white to red to deep purple. He wanted to scream something at me, but it never came. He just glared instead, then stormed out. The rest had a little glare too, the lieutenant, the sergeant-major, the sergeant and the corporal. But the more I rattle them, the more I fancy my chances of getting out.'

After that first date at the Van Morrison concert, Sorcha went out regularly with Frank. He took her to places she had never thought of visiting before, the theatre, art exhibitions and poetry readings. He also began to tell her about how Northern Ireland was changing.

'O'Neill's a good man, I know he's a unionist, but he sees change must happen. The bigots must not be allowed to stop him. We'll have to put on a bit of pressure from our side.'

Frank went to meetings of the Northern Ireland Civil Rights Association – NICRA – and told Sorcha about their objectives: to define the basic rights of citizens; to protect the rights of the individual; to demand guarantees of freedom of speech, assembly and association; and to inform the public of their lawful rights. Frank, with other students, went on protests all over the north to highlight discrimination and campaign for civil rights. He talked to Sorcha about the students all over the world who were tearing down the old order and trying to build a new and better society.

The liberation forces in Vietnam launched their Tet offensive and brought that conflict into the world's spotlight. Protest movements against the war mushroomed, and in Belfast Sorcha and Frank helped to organise a picket on the John Wayne propaganda film, 'The Green Berets'.

'Sorcha! Will you look at this!'

She was washing up in the back kitchen when she heard her ma call and hurried through. Her ma sat watching the TV and pointed to the screen as Sorcha entered. It looked like a riot, but Sorcha gasped as she saw it was the police who were rioting. A solid group of peelers strode down a street lashing out with riot batons at anyone who got in the way. There had been a civil rights demonstration in Londonderry, the commentator said, and the RUC had cleared the streets. Later that night, radio reports said sporadic trouble was continuing between the RUC and 'young hooligans' from the Bogside.

Sorcha knew Frank had intended to go to Derry for the protest and was worried about what might have happened to him. The image of the police violence kept flashing through her mind and she tried to make sense of what had happened. She remembered her granda speaking scathingly of the Free Staters who had taken the British bait in 1921, and accepted the partition of the country in exchange for a measure of independence for the south. The nationalist minority in the six counties were abandoned to the tender mercies of the new unionist state of Northern Ireland, which remained part of the United Kingdom.

The unionists, descendants of the settlers, were still afraid of the native Irish, and with British backing they had set about constructing a sectarian state. Lord Craigavon, Northern Ireland's first prime minister, stated: 'I have always said that I am an Orangeman first and a member of this parliament afterwards... all I boast is that we have a Protestant parliament and a Protestant state.'

Religion became the badge that indicated one's origins and allegiances: Protestants were the chosen people and loyal, Catholics were outcasts and not to be trusted. Catholics were discriminated against in jobs and housing, and were kept in line by an armed police force, the Royal Ulster Constabulary, backed up by the B-Specials, an armed loyalist militia. Also, the British army kept soldiers in the province in a string of barracks throughout the area. The infamous Special Powers Act was brought in to allow the RUC and B-men to deal with any troublemakers.

Sorcha did not hear from Frank till one evening a few days after the Derry troubles. He was very excited and told her about what had happened in Derry, impatiently brushing aside her retort that she had been worried he might have been hurt.

'No way,' he said grinning, and told her about the series of protests organised by the students after the RUC actions against the civil rights march. On Sunday they had marched to the home of the minister of home affairs, Mr Craig, who claimed that the IRA had been behind the Derry march and denied that the RUC had been brutal in dealing with the marchers.

But Frank was most excited when he told Sorcha about that day's events. 'We got lots and lots of students from Queens and we marched on the city hall, there were thousands of us. They wouldn't let us in so we sat down in Linenhall Street for hours and hours. There were so many of us they couldn't do anything, and in the end they let in a delegation to protest about the police in Derry.'

Frank went on to relate how after the students had returned to the university they had held a meeting and formed their own organisation, People's Democracy. He reeled off the new group's demands: one man one vote; a fair drawing of electoral boundaries; freedom of speech and assembly; repeal of the Special Powers Act; and a fair allocation of jobs and housing.

'We needed a new group,' Frank explained. 'NICRA are all right and there's a lot of good people in it, but some of the older ones keep wanting to put the brake on everything. Now we've got PD off the ground we can keep our foot on the accelerator.'

On the news that night they showed the protest at the City Hall, and they also said that the Reverend Ian Paisley and his wife had met the home affairs minister at Stormont. Paisley was interviewed afterwards. 'The Ulster people have expressed their point of view... no surrender and no comment,' he said.

'It's too late now for us to get to the local cafe, so we might just as well go to the beer tent and get a few bevvys in,' Neil said to Billy. They were both on cookhouse duties which included washing up after the evening meal and preparing the eating area for breakfast next morning.

As they entered the beer tent and went towards the bar they passed Sergeant McNair who was surrounded by a group of soldiers whom he was regaling with stories of his battle exploits. The sergeant had a loud voice and Neil and Billy had no trouble hearing the unfolding of his tales.

'Look at the state of this country since the nig-nogs took over! When we were in control we didn't stand for no fucking about. During the aggro here I was stationed at Nanyuki. I remember this area well, it was what we called a free fire zone. What that meant was, if you caught any black bastards in it you could shoot them dead. Well we was crafty, I was a lance corporal then, and me and this sergeant we knew you could get a fiver for a terrorist dead or alive. So we used to go on sambo hunts and many's a piss up we had on the proceeds. I remember one day we'd gone out and we stopped the truck 'cause we'd seen a movement behind a bush. I was just about to shoot when the sarge said to stop, and he went in and pulled them out. It wasn't a man see, it was a young jungle bunny. Not bad looking for one of them either. Well we thought waste not want not, so we ripped her gear off – I always remember she didn't have knickers like our birds wear, frilly and that, hers were more like our PT shorts. But she had the same equipment all right. The sarge he bagged first go and then we all took a turn, except for this one squaddie who said he didn't want to, must have been a poof or something.'

Sergeant McNair laughed loudly at his own joke, then continued, 'It made a change for paying for it from those fucking black whores – did you know what we found out about them? Well we wondered how some of those Mau-Mau fuckers in the hills were getting ammunition, then we discovered that the whores were servicing some of our blokes and charging five bullets for a jump like. The stupid fuckers were paying it too, then the rounds were smuggled up to the black bastards in the hills.'

The sergeant shook his head. 'Well, anyway I was for shooting this jungle bunny after we had fucked her – we could have got another fiver for a dead terrorist. But the sarge, he must have taken a case of the softs and he said to let her go, still I suppose we got a good screw out of it.'

Like everyone else, Neil had listened in silence, but now he said softly to Billy, 'I wonder how they would feel if a black army did the same in Britain as we did in this country? The funny thing is how friendly the blacks in that village are to us, yet it's only eight years since the war ended here. Come on, let's get out of here. I'm fed up listening to that fucker, he's as thick as pigshit and twice as smelly.'

Neil and Billy drank up, pushed back their chairs and made for the tent flap. As they passed Sergeant McNair's table Neil made a motion with his hand as if it were an aeroplane and made a noise to match.

'Airoowo! ... Veroom! ... Kapow! Kapow! Swing the lights, it's Sergeant McNair and warrie time again. You should write down some of your stories, sarge, you could be the army's answer to Enid Blyton.'

Sergeant McNair looked up, flushed by the interruption. 'Well, well, look who it is, Danny the red. I hear you're trying to get out again, McKinnon. What use would you be in civvy street? Have you got a soap-box booked at Hyde Park Corner? Or will you fuck off back to Russia where you belong?'

Neil grinned down at the sergeant. 'Actually I've just heard something that makes me want to stay in and become a good soldier like you, sarge. Seemingly the British people want to honour all sergeants and above for their good services by burying them in Whitehall when they die. I think that's a great gesture. The only trouble is they are going to have to bury them upright, rather than flat.'

Sergeant McNair's eyes narrowed as he watched Neil continue towards the exit. He knew he shouldn't ask but curiosity and the drink overruled his better judgement. 'And why should they bury them that way? Is it to get them all in?' he asked.

Neil turned grinning from the tent flap, 'No that wasn't it. They want to bury yous upright – 'cause they want to use your heads as cobblestones. Night, night.'

Back in the tent Neil told Billy why he had changed his attitude towards the army. 'It was in Aden like, I'd just been made up, got my second stripe and keen with it. It was just like what happened here, we really gave those Arabs some stick and I was reckoned to be good at it, dishing out the aggro. Well, we were sent out this night to get this bloke, we were told he was responsible for some of our blokes getting the chop. We were to sort him out – they said don't bother to bring him back, just do him, but no gunfire if it could be helped.'

Neil shook his head and looked across at Billy. 'We found where he lived, this shack, and kicked down the door. There he was in the middle of the room, he started to jabber away, we just piled into him, kicking and hitting him. My mate got him with his rifle butt and he went down, we really kicked the shit out of him then, no one wanted to say stop. We eventually stopped out of exhaustion, he was in a right bloody state, as dead as a door nail. We stared at him for a minute then we started to file out. I was the last to leave and as I was going I heard a noise, it came from behind this curtain covering a cupboard. I leapt across the room and ripped it back and there they were – it was the bloke's fucking wife and two little kids. Well, my leg came back and my boot started forward, I was going to kick them to pieces too, when it stopped inches from her gut. It was her eyes that did it, they just stared at me. She didn't try to defend herself, but her eyes, there was fear and horror in them but there was defiance and contempt there too. I just looked at her and the kids, then I got out of there like a bat out of hell. After that it was all downhill as far as me and the army was concerned.'

A week before the exercise ended Neil was told that this time his discharge had come through and for the sum of £200 he would be a free man.

'Good riddance to bad rubbish,' was the sergeant major's comment as he arranged for Neil to go back on the first available flight.

When he had packed his gear for his departure Neil turned to Billy. 'Well stay lucky, all the best and remember the old saying: "Old soldiers never die, but the bastards will get a few young ones killed, if you give them half a chance."'

That night as Billy lay in the tent thinking of Neil and wondering how he would make out in civvy street, he found himself remembering the version of the Engelbert Humperdink hit that Neil used to sing:

> Please release me let me go,
> For I don't love the army anymore,
> To keep me in would be a sin,
> So release me and let me live again.

Sorcha was washing the tea things in the back kitchen when she heard her ma answer a familiar knock on the door.

'Come away in Teresa,' she heard her ma say, and then there was the sound of the two women talking urgently. It sounds as if something has happened, Sorcha thought, and then her ma poked her head round the door.

'It's Teresa – can you make us some tea?' she asked, and then seeing the questioning look on Sorcha's face added, 'It's her man, you know he was working across the water, like your da? Well he's had an accident.'

Sorcha filled the kettle and switched it on, then finished washing and drying the dishes. She then made a pot of tea, put it on a tray with the cups and sugar and milk and a few biscuits and carried it through to the living room. Tears stained Teresa McCann's face as she told Sorcha's ma about what had happened.

'It was some demolition crowd he worked for, I got a telegram this afternoon saying there had been a bit of an accident.

They gave a number to ring, and I ran out to use the phone at the wee shop.' Teresa burst into tears.

Sorcha poured out the tea while her ma comforted Teresa who took a sip of tea, then continued, 'I got through to the crowd he worked for, they said he'd been on demolishing a building and he'd had a bad fall. He'd been up a good height and he'd taken a bad knock on the head.' Her tears started again.

Sorcha's ma said she would just go and check that the McCann children were all right. Sorcha poured out second cups of tea and looked across at Teresa's face with the tears dripping down. I hope he will pull through, she thought, remembering Teresa's husband. His name was Liam but everyone called him Spoons. He would hold two large spoons in his right hand and knock out a tune by rattling them against the palm of his left hand.

'A dab hand at the spoons,' people had said, and after a while that became his name. They said he liked a drink, and so he did, but he always sent money home every week .

'As regular as clockwork,' Teresa had said.

If he was badly hurt it would be a big blow: there were five youngsters with the three eldest at school. Sorcha thought of Gerry the oldest boy who had a bad chest; she often fetched medicine for him as she passed through the city centre every day.

Her ma returned to say the children were okay. Next door were in looking after them and she'd arranged with other neighbours to take it in turns to look in over the next few days till Teresa got sorted out.

In an attempt to take Teresa's mind off the accident, Sorcha's ma started to recall the days when she and Teresa had gone to school together.

'We both left on the same day. We got jobs in one of the mills that was still open, it didn't last long before it was closed down too. I wouldn't recommend the work 'cause it was terrible, but we did have a laugh, us two together and the rest of the girls.'

Frank had gone home to his parents that Christmas but came to visit Sorcha in the bookshop just afterwards. He told her about People's Democracy's latest plans.

'We're fed up hanging back listening to promises, so we've organised a march from Belfast to Derry, starting on the first of January.'

Frank explained that the idea behind the march came from the Black civil rights freedom marches through America's deep south. The objectives were similar also, to expose the prejudiced sectarian nature of the state, hoping this would force the central government to intervene and bring in reforms.

The next Wednesday Sorcha went to the city hall to see Frank and the other students off. She had made a few sandwiches which she thrust into Frank's hands as she waved goodbye. There were so few, Sorcha thought, less than a hundred, with the 'one man – one vote' banner up the front. They hardly seemed to pose a threat to the state, but at the other side of the square a large contingent of loyalists were gathered waving union jacks and chanting 'one taig – no vote.'

On the TV news that night it said that the PD march was experiencing opposition along its route and that a memorial to Roddy McCorley, a leader of the 1798 rebellion, had been blown up in Toomebridge. There were similar reports each subsequent night until Saturday when it was reported that many of the marchers had been injured at Burntollet bridge. The announcer also stated that riots had ensued when the march had at last reached Derry and that the prime minister Terence O'Neill had issued a statement calling the marchers 'foolhardy and irresponsible'. 'Enough is enough,' he said. 'We have heard sufficient for now about civil rights... let us hear a little about civic responsibility.'

On the Monday Frank walked into the bookshop and Sorcha gasped when she saw the white bandage wrapped around the top of his head. He grinned when he saw her alarm.

'Just a scratch, we copped it at Burntollet,' he said.

He told her about the march, how right from the start the RUC had tried to divert the civil rights marchers towards loyalist counter-demonstrators. Sometimes, the marchers had reached safety only by breaking through the police lines. The peelers had achieved their objective at Burntollet by leading them into a well laid ambush at the bridge. Many of the attackers that day were off-duty B-Specials, and some of the police who were supposed to be protecting the march had turned round and joined in the assaults on the marchers.

A somewhat battered and depleted group of marchers, Frank among them, had insisted on continuing on to Derry. Even there, the peelers kept holding up the procession at various places while loyalists bombarded the marchers with bricks and stones. Eventually the march reached the Guildhall Square and a rapturous welcome from a large nationalist crowd. That night a group of peelers, evidently upset that the march had got through, attacked the Bogside area, smashing windows, kicking doors and attacking anyone they met.

Some Bogsiders had told Frank about it. 'The peelers were pissed out of their minds, crying drunk so they were,' they said, and went on to explain that the RUC men had been singing a song they'd made up based on the Monkees' hit:

Hey, hey, we're the Monkees,
And we'll monkey you around,
'Till your blood is flowing on the ground.

Part Three

1969
Something in the air

Some said the flames were Ulster's own,

And more they were extraneous,

But a Down man swore they lit their lone,

That combustion was spontaneous.

Brian na Banban (A Bonfire On The Border)

...last night another soldier...

Clonard: Bernadette speaks

'Sorcha! Come quick – look at this.' The urgent shout brought her running through from the shop to the small yard at the rear. Victor was pointing to the clouds and Sorcha looking up saw a spot of brilliant light moving across the hazy afternoon sky. The bright spot continued its progress for a few more minutes then burst apart, splitting into smaller pieces which fell to earth. That night the TV news said a meteorite had passed over Northern Ireland before breaking up and falling. A piece had smashed through the roof of an RUC armament depot near Lisburn. The news also said that five hundred British troops had flown in to be on standby and that an explosion had cut a water main supplying Belfast creating a serious shortage.

Three days later Terence O'Neill resigned as prime minister, taking with him any hope of reforms. Now the civil rights movement was locked into direct conflict with the Northern Ireland state. The explosion on the water pipe had been one of a series carried out clandestinely by the UVF, a loyalist paramilitary organisation. They hoped the IRA would be blamed and that this would harden the attitudes of the unionist population. Soon afterwards another civil rights protest in Derry was attacked by loyalists, and in the riot which followed the RUC once again forced their way into the Bogside. This time the peelers broke into houses and assaulted the residents; one, Samuel Devenny, who was severely beaten, would die three months later.

Sorcha had thought that Frank would have been upset with O'Neill going, but he just grinned when she mentioned it.

'Sure we all realised we'd never get any change out of him, but now it's gone past all that anyway. It's the British we have to convince now. If we can get through to them and they say jump, then the crowd here will have to obey and in double quick time too.'

Sorcha looked at Frank and held up the paper that had been lying on the counter. 'I see Bernadette made her first speech in the House of Commons,' she said.

'Yes, she was great, she really socked it to them,' responded Frank, beaming.

Sorcha spread out the paper. To her Bernadette seemed to represent the ethos of their generation in the North. A woman who had struggled through adversity, who bowed her head to no-one, who kept pressing forward. Suddenly Sorcha remembered a saying from James Connolly that her granda had always quoted: 'The great appear great because we are on our knees – let us rise.'

Well, in Bernadette Devlin they had a woman who was off her knees, and Sorcha softly spoke the last words from the end of the new MP's speech in the Commons. 'I am not speaking about one night of broken glass – but of fifty years of human misery.'

'Wake up, you lazy bastard.'

He felt the boot thud into his side and snapped awake.

'You're supposed to be on guard.' The second lieutenant was standing over Billy glaring down at him.

He had been posted to a unit in Germany and was in the middle of exercise 'Red Menace', one of the frequent schemes that the NATO forces indulged in.

'Sorry sir, it won't happen again,' Billy said. He straightened himself into a lookout position, pushed his rifle forward, and tried to look alert while lying on the ground.

'It had better not, I'll be back,' said the officer menacingly before moving off to check the other sentries.

They had been on the go now for forty-eight hours without sleep, and the sun beating down had proved too big a temptation. Billy bit his lip. I must stay awake, he thought. He knew that he had been recommended for promotion from his last unit but he realised he would have to prove himself here in Germany too. He looked around trying to find something that would hold his attention and keep him awake. He concentrated his gaze on the distant buildings of a town where the outline of a castle took his eye. Where they were Billy neither knew nor cared, but as he stared at the castle he suddenly remembered the conversation of the two Germans he had met the previous day.

The unit had been passing in convoy through the town when they had stopped for some reason for a short time. Billy and the two other squaddies had realised their good luck as their landrover and trailer had parked outside a Gasthaus. They hadn't dared enter the pub but had found an open window where two Germans were sitting inside talking and drinking. The soldiers had engaged the Germans in conversation and persuaded them to buy beers, which the squaddies had drunk furtively while keeping an eye open for officers or NCOs. The Germans had obviously been drinking for some time, and one of them who spoke good English insisted on telling the soldiers the history of the town.

As Billy stared at the castle he recalled the story the German had told about it. In that castle four centuries ago Martin Luther, the leader of the Protestant reformation in Germany, had met Huldreich Zwingli, the founder of the reformation in Zurich. Under the tutelage of the local ruler Philip of Hess, they argued out their respective theories on the sacrament. Both dismissed the Catholic doctrine which held that the wine and the bread are transformed into the blood and body of Jesus at at the moment of consecration. Zwingli argued that the bread and wine merely represented the body and blood of Christ. Luther on the other hand claimed that the sacrament was both things at once: that the body and the blood existed 'in, with and under' the bread and wine. To conclude his argument Luther quoted Jesus's statement, 'take, eat, this is my body.' Taking a piece of chalk, Luther wrote 'this is my body' on a table, drew a circle round it and sat down.

The two Germans had then started discussing the role of Luther and his new religion. Protestantism had become established as the main religion in the country and they both agreed that most of the people had welcomed the reformation. But later the peasants had rebelled against the feudal power of the princes and both sides in the conflict had looked to Luther for moral support. After some deliberation Luther had chosen to side with the princes and the status quo, and the peasant revolt was suppressed.

The Germans argued over whether Luther had been right while the squaddies had listened politely, if a little bemused. But as one of them said afterwards, 'We don't give a toss for Luther, the town or the castle, but we'd listen to any waffle as long as the krauts are getting the beers in.'

Billy could feel sleep threaten to overcome him again and was vigorously rubbing his eyes when he heard stealthy footsteps to his left. Instantly becoming alert, he shouted out the challenge.

'Well done, glad to see you're still awake,' said the second lieutenant sarcastically, striding up to stand at Billy's side.

That evening the officers gave a briefing for the mock battle that was to be the culmination of the exercise. The regiment who were the blue force would be allowed two hours sleep, then would move in attack formation to a distant wooded ridge where the enemy red force, a Guards unit, were dug in. The officers related a tale from the history of the regiment centuries before when on some foreign field the same Guards unit had broken before an enemy charge and ran, leaving the regiment to fend by themselves.

'Now's our chance to get even, to get our own back,' the officers said. 'We want you to go in hard, we'll back you even if there's a few cracked heads as long as you win.'

After the officers left, the NCOs went round telling the soldiers that they would be fighting for Scottish honour, and that the

Guards were English poofs who had been heard saying nasty things about the men of the regiment.

That night, exercise 'Red Menace' culminated in a battle royal on the ridge, with casualties on both sides. The umpires took some time to untangle the two units before declaring the fight a draw. The regiment suffered two men with broken legs and one with a smashed ankle, while the Guards had one man with a fractured arm, one with broken ribs and one with a cracked skull. None of the men from either unit knew that the previous evening all the officers on the exercise had gathered for a drink. An argument had ensued about which unit had the toughest men and bets had been wagered between the officers of the regiment and those of the Guards about the outcome of the final battle the next night.

'We're looking for volunteers, Charlie.'

Sorcha had gone to the corner shop for milk and a man from the area had entered behind her and started talking to the shopkeeper.

'Some of us think we should be doing something to protect the area, just in case.' As he continued Sorcha recognised the speaker as a man who lived at the end of the street.

The shopkeeper looked surprised. 'I'll just serve the girl here,' he said, and went to get the milk.

'Surely we'll be all right,' he continued as Sorcha paid for the milk.

'Well, Ardoyne had a wee skirmish with the peelers. I'm told the orangies in the Shankill have got themselves together, it could be us next.' The man was still trying to convince the shopkeeper as Sorcha left the shop.

Next day when Sorcha met Frank she told him of the conversation she had overheard in the shop.

'There too, eh!' he said. 'I heard they've set up a defence committee in the Bogside. Everyone's waiting to see if they ban the apprentice boys' march in Derry. They've banned all our civil rights marches in city centres for the past year, but you can bet they won't ban their own crowd. If it goes ahead there's bound to be trouble, but the Bogsiders are saying the peelers won't get into their area again.'

Tension remained high throughout nationalist areas as, on the twelfth of August 1969, fifteen thousand unionists assembled in Derry. Many, with orange sashes and carrying rolled umbrellas, wore their best Sunday suits and bowler hats. They had come to commemorate an event that had taken place two hundred and eighty years before when a group of Protestant apprentice boys had shut the city gates in the face of the Catholic King James. The march celebrated the settlers' ascendancy over the native Irish, and, as predicted, a riot developed as the marchers passed close to the Bogside.

The RUC protecting the march baton-charged the Bogsiders, expecting to drive them back as usual and wreak havoc in the area. But this time the people had built barricades and stockpiled petrol bombs, which they used to keep the hated peelers at bay. The RUC soon introduced a new weapon of their own, CS gas, firing volley after volley into the nationalist ghetto area. The battle of the Bogside commenced in earnest, with the smell of burning and CS gas hanging in the air, and would only end forty-eight hours later when British soldiers marched into the front line in place of a tired and demoralised RUC.

In Clonard, like other nationalist areas across the province, the people listened to the news bulletins on the radio and in the evening watched events on TV. Sorcha phoned Victor from the shop to say she would not be going in to work that day.

'People think there may be trouble around here after what's happening in Derry,' she told him. But she did not mention that barricades were already being erected at street ends, and little knots of people were gathered here and there frantically discussing events. As Sorcha walked back from the shop she paused by one such group to hear what the word was.

'They're shipping bus loads of peelers into Derry. We've got to step it up here, keep the bastards stretched,' one man said.

'But what have we got to defend ourselves with?' another interjected. He turned to the man from the end of the street whom Sorcha had seen speaking to the shopkeeper about defending the area. 'Will your crowd have arms?' he asked. 'We'll need them if the B-men join the orangies in an attack.'

The man from the end of the street looked embarrassed. 'We've got nothing, we haven't even got a fucking peashooter,' he answered, then shrugged his shoulders. 'With the crowd in charge now, it's like pissing into the wind asking for anything.'

'That's a big fucking help. What's the use of the IRA if it hasn't any fucking guns?' the man who had asked the question muttered angrily.

'Let's keep it calm and look at what we can do,' the first speaker cut in quickly. 'We'll make the barricades as strong as we can, but put something in them that will make them burn – old tyres, stuff like that. We'll defend them with whatever we've got – sticks, stones and molotovs. If we can't hold them and we get driven back, then we can set fire to them. At least the other crowd won't get past or make use of them then.'

Sorcha was listening intently when she felt a tugging on her arm. She turned and saw it was young Gerry McCann. He had been running and was wheezing as he fought to get his breath; he still couldn't get any words out but pointed with his hand. Sorcha looked and could barely conceal a gasp as she saw the clouds of black smoke rising over the rooftops. The men had turned to look too and one exclaimed, 'It's the bottom of the Falls!'

Soon the word came through that crowds from the Shankill had attacked down Percy, Dover and Northumberland Streets. B-Specials with guns had backed the loyalists who forced their way into Divis Street where they planted a union jack. In Northumberland Street the advance was halted by nationalists. The defenders, from behind a barricade of burning tyres in Albert Street, showered the disused old mill building across the road with petrol bombs till it erupted into flames so fierce they effectively blocked any passage through. The loyalists fell back but proceeded to systematically set fire to all the nationalist homes at the lower end of Percy and Dover Streets.

That night, in Clonard, the early news was greeted with cheers and yells: the siege of the Bogside was over. The RUC had withdrawn and British troops were passively holding the line. Now that the government in London was directly involved surely things must change, people thought.

The tension in Belfast, however, continued to rise, especially when the distinctive sound of Browning heavy machine guns was heard. All day RUC Shoreland armoured cars, fitted with these guns, had appeared along the Falls, menacing nationalists. Now, as if driven mad by the news from Derry, they had opened fire on the Divis flats. The machine-gun bullets tore through the jerry-built flats like a knife through butter, killing a nine-year-old boy called Patrick Rooney and a young British soldier home on leave.

That night the defenders posted lookouts and remained at the ready, drinking the gallons of scalding hot tea provided by the women. The next morning the word was yelled through the area that British soldiers had marched onto the Falls Road and taken up positions facing the Shankill. Later faces began to get anxious again: the troops had not advanced but were rigidly holding to their positions at the bottom of the road.

Suddenly a whisper went around: 'The Mackies crowd are leaving early.' Mackies was a heavy engineering factory on the edge of Clonard which, like others of its type, employed an almost totally Protestant workforce. Now, for some reason, those workers were silently streaming away early along the Springfield Road. Once again knots of people filled the narrow streets talking agitatedly, now and again casting anxious glances in the direction of the Shankill.

Suddenly a single brick spun in a lazy arch over the roofs of Bombay Street. The defenders stood as if rooted to the spot as the brick completed its flight and crashed into the middle of the road-way. Breaking in two on impact, one half of the brick flopped over to lie still while the other half bounced on into the gutter. The people of Clonard still stood motionless, when a yell from many throats rent the air: 'No surrender! Up the Shankill! Fuck the pope!'

A hail of stones, bottles and bricks now followed the trajectory of the first one over the roofs and into Bombay Street. This second volley broke the spell and the defenders snapped into action, answering the incoming hail of missiles with outgoing volleys of their own. The battle raged with the nationalists desperately holding their own, beating off several direct assaults. Then gunshots were heard from adjoining streets and a slow retreat started. The whisper went around that off-duty RUC and B-men had joined the loyalists and were using their guns to help the attack.

Sorcha went to visit her granny to make sure the old lady wasn't too scared, but she was most indignant at the thought.

'Scared!' she exclaimed scathingly. 'We went through much worse in the past. When your granda was alive we had the peelers here so often I almost charged them lodging money.'

When Sorcha returned and slipped inside the house her ma looked at her grimly. 'They've just shot a wee lad in Waterville Street. They say it's bad, he didn't stand a chance the poor wee soul, stones against guns.' Her ma shook her head. 'We'd better be ready to bail out, in case they come pouring down here.'

But the people of Clonard had fought desperately, making any advance hard going for the loyalist crowd, the bulk of whom seemed contented to set fire to the houses along Bombay Street where they had gained the ascendancy. As the defenders waited tensely, looking in horror at the flames and smoke from the burning homes, a cry went up from behind, 'The tommies are coming, the tommies are coming,' and soon a file of British soldiers could be seen treading slowly up the road. The loyalists headed off, gloating over a good day's work, as the troops came slowly past the barricades to take up positions, silhouetted against the burning houses in Bombay Street.

Later Sorcha and her ma took blankets and some tinned food down to the hall in Hawthorn Street where some of the families from the burned homes were being looked after. Sorcha stared in horror at the groups of mainly women and children who were looking about them with glazed eyes. Many had not been able to save any belongings except for the clothes they stood in. Some were talking of moving down south where it was said the Free Staters were setting up refugee camps.

The next day the smoking ruins of the houses in Bombay Street stood as monuments to the predicament of the nationalist community in the Northern Ireland state. They were there on sufferance, to be at best tolerated, but if they got uppity then retribution such as this would be the result. Fifty families had lost their homes in this small street alone and the people of Clonard contemplated the situation.

The old ones had seen or heard about such situations before but the young had been traumatised. They had been horrified and frightened, but now were angry. The lad who had been shot had died: one of their own had made the supreme sacrifice in defence of their area. People said he'd been in the Fianna, the IRA youth movement, and a few days later the people of the area followed him on his last journey to Milltown. It was the first of many such journeys to bury fallen republican fighters in that cemetery in the years to come.

In Clonard animated discussions took place in the houses and on the streets. 'What will happen next?' was the question on everyone's lips. At the moment the British soldiers would probably keep the loyalists away, but could they be trusted? After all, the Irish had been fighting them for hundreds of years so they appeared to be strange allies. The word came from Derry that James Callaghan, the home secretary, who on behalf of the British Labour government had sent the troops in, had appeared in the Bogside and made promises about things to come. Some people said that now the British were directly involved the situation would soon be sorted out. 'They can't let things carry on as they are,' they said.

Others said that people would be wise not to expect too much from the Brits. 'Sure, but don't all politicians make promises – putting them into practice is another matter, and hasn't Callaghan gone and made promises to the other crowd too?'

With the houses in Bombay Street still smoking, the people knew the only ones they could really trust were themselves. The defence committee passed the word around that the barricades would stay and would be guarded round the clock. Street committees were formed to carry out the day-to-day running of the area: Clonard had become a liberated zone.

Sorcha went back to work the next week and when she came home the first evening she found her ma fiddling with the radio

dial. Suddenly the programme came through loud and clear.

'This is Radio Free Belfast. I have a request here from the people of the Bogside in Derry to their nationalist brothers and sisters in Belfast: Thunderclap Newman, with "Something in the Air".'

Billy flinched and kept his face and body pressed to the ground as he heard the whine of machine-gun bullets passing overhead. They were slowly crawling forward over ditches and under rolls of barbed wire. Now and again, as the soldiers passed small sand-bagged enclosures, a small charge of explosives would go off with an earsplitting crack, showering the closest men with sand. The unit was at a battle-training range where the men experienced live-firing conditions, threw hand grenades and fired anti-tank missiles.

Sergeant Wallace, who was the NCO in charge of Billy's section, fancied himself as a bit of a poet, and as he marched them back and forward from the various ranges he used to make up couplets for the soldiers to chant:

Left, right – left, right
When in doubt – kick a kraut.
Left, right – left, right
Feeling krank – have a wank.

Life for the squaddies in Germany consisted of periods of boring training in the big old German army barracks, broken up with exercises in the countryside. The officers constantly drummed into the men that they were the first line of defence of the free world against the totalitarian menace that threatened across the border of a divided Germany. Social life for the squaddies revolved around drinking in the NAAFI or the little clubs that sprang up in some barracks selling cheap drink. Many also visited the bierkellers in the local town where the men of the regiment quickly became feared and to a large extent shunned by the local population, who coined the nickname 'poisoned dwarfs', for the soldiers.

The squaddies proudly boasted about their past exploits against the 'krauts', as the Germans were known. Billy's new mates told him about their visit to West Berlin on an exercise earlier in the year. They had flown in and, completing their part in the manoeuvres, gone on a piss-up in the city. On the way back to camp, drunk out of their minds, they had come upon a large monument dedicated to the reunification of the country. In the middle of the monument a flame burned, to be kept lit until Germany was united again. The temptation proved too great and the squaddies climbed the monument en masse and gathered around the flame to piss on it till it went out.

One day Sergeant Wallace called Billy into the section office. 'I've good news,' he said. 'We're thinking of making you up to lance corporal, first step up the ladder.' The sergeant winked at Billy. 'I've put in a good word for you. So let's keep our fingers crossed, eh.'

A few weeks later Billy was sent on a cadre course to prepare him to be an NCO. It consisted of different lectures, as well as training in giving drill orders and a few endurance tests. The last test was to be one where all the men on the course were let loose in a country area and soldiers from another unit would try to track them down. Billy and a friend managed to stay free most of the day, but in the early evening they were ambushed and captured by a corporal and three men from the pursuing unit. Their hands were tied behind their backs and they were pushed into the back of a landrover. Billy recognised one of his captors as a soldier who sometimes drank in the same bierkeller in the town and asked him if they were being taken back to barracks.

'It's supposed to be a secret,' the soldier whispered back to him. 'But we have to hand you over to some other bods who are going to interrogate yous. They've taken over an old farmhouse and that's where we're headed.'

When Billy asked who these others were, the soldier just shook his head. 'Don't know mate, mystery men. Though I did hear they'd just flown in from Blighty.'

Billy felt a sense of foreboding but quickly threw it off: they were bound to be back in barracks before dark, he thought. He certainly hoped so, as he hadn't eaten all day and was feeling famished.

At the old farmhouse Billy and his friend were pushed out into the arms of a number of tough-looking men in tight-fitting boiler suits. Billy found himself propelled forward towards an outbuilding with the men screaming in his ear to double up. When they reached the building, Billy was forced onto his knees and ordered to do squat-ups. He struggled to comply but when, with his hands tied behind him, he found it difficult to keep his balance, one of the men roughly grabbed his hair and hauled him up and down.

After what seemed like hundreds of squats and with his legs aching, Billy felt a boot in his back propel him forward, and he fell flat with his face in a mud pool. As he spluttered and spat out the muddy water, his hands were untied and he was ordered to do press-ups, until he lost count of how many he had done and could barely raise himself off the ground. He was dragged to his feet and pushed to the outbuilding wall against which he had to stand spreadeagled on his toes with his outstretched finger-tips touching. Billy was then searched, while all the time the men screamed abuse in his ears, pushing and shoving him if he moved a fraction.

After what seemed like hours of being forced to do various strenuous exercises in turn, two of the men grabbed Billy's arms while the third kicked open the door of the outbuilding. It was dark inside except for a single bright spotlight which shone on a prisoner. Billy felt his heart go cold. The building was an old byre and the prisoner was in a stall, his upstretched arms held in place by shackles hanging from the rafters. The man looked in a dreadful state: his torn shirt revealed angry weals across his chest, blood was caked around an area of his scalp and one eye was half-closed and bruised-looking. As the prisoner sagged forward looking more than half dead, the third interrogator strolled up to him and screamed into his ear, 'Are you going to tell us now, you fucking turd?'

There was no response from the prisoner and the interrogator grabbed him roughly by the hair. Billy's vision was now obscured by the interrogator's back, but he saw the raised hand and heard the crack as the prisoner was struck a heavy blow to the face. The interrogator stepped back and Billy could see the blood streaming from the prisoner's mouth, dripping down to soak his shirtfront. The interrogator pointed at the prisoner. 'This fucker's finished, he's as good as snuffed it, take him down – and chain up the other fucker.'

The prisoner collapsed when unchained and had to be carried out as Billy was shackled up in his place.

'We'll be back for you shortly, you'll wish you'd never been born,' snarled the interrogator into Billy's ear. Then they all left, slamming the door as they went.

By the next morning Billy was completely exhausted, frightened and very hungry too. The interrogators had kept returning at intervals through the night to continue their bombardment, subjecting Billy to physical exercises and making him stand spreadeagled against the wall, then chaining him up again and all the time screaming abuse in his ears. At any minute he was expecting to be badly beaten, but so far he remained unbruised. Suddenly the door crashed open again and the main interrogator entered. Billy braced himself for more abuse but this time the man smiled.

'Well done, son,' he said, as he unchained Billy. 'You can go back to your barracks now and get some shuteye. You did well, better than a lot of your mates, they'd have been singing like canaries if they'd had anything to tell.'

Billy felt as if he had just woken from a bad nightmare as he stumbled out the door after the man. Outside the interrogator pointed to the truck that would take them back to barracks.

'There you are – I hope you won't take it personal, we're only doing our job, same as you.'

Billy felt his anger rising up. 'But what about that poor bastard you beat up?' he exclaimed.

The interrogator grinned and pointed across at a group of men. 'You mean him? He's one of ours,' he said.

Billy looked in astonishment, it was the same man who had been chained up in the stall, but now he looked as right as rain, no cuts, no bruises and no sign of blood.

The interrogator laughed. 'It's the same as they use in the movies, we paint it on. It had you fooled, eh?'

Billy looked closely at the interrogator. 'But the blood? I saw you hit him,' he gasped.

The interrogator laughed again. 'A blood blister they call it, it's a blood substitute in a little bag. He had it in his mouth and when I pretended to smack him he bit it and it gushed out.'

The interrogator smiled at Billy again and held out his hand. 'Shake on it – just to show there's no hard feelings,' he said.

Billy was about to grasp the hand when the soldier who had been captured with him was led crying from another building towards the truck. The interrogator followed Billy's gaze. 'I'm afraid your friend didn't do so well, we broke him down,' he said.

Billy looked at the man's outstretched hand, then walked slowly towards the truck. As he boarded the vehicle Billy heard the angry voice of the interrogator shout after him.

'If you think it's bad what we did to yous, you should see what we do when we get our hands on a real enemy.'

In the old days the invaders, secure in their castle at the bottom of what was to become the Falls Road, watched the surrounding countryside suspiciously. Sometimes parties of native Irish would suddenly appear out of the forests and stand on the Cluan-Ard, the high meadow, gazing sullenly down at the castle and the invaders within.

The castle is long gone, but now a new generation of soldiers from over the sea confronted the people of Clonard. At first relations were cordial; locals feared repeats of the loyalist attacks that had gutted Bombay Street and the troops started to build a fence as protection. Some soldiers quickly got on speaking terms with some local residents, and the British government announced that the hated B-Specials were to be disbanded and the RUC was to patrol without arms. While this strengthened the feeling of security in nationalist areas, it enraged the loyalists and led to a series of clashes along the Shankill Road during which the RUC sustained their first fatal casualty in this round of the troubles. The British army went in to quell these protests, shooting two loyalists dead in the process.

Sorcha had continued to go to work, each day passing out through the barricades and passing back in again at night. She saw Frank infrequently as he and his friends in PD were working in overdrive producing leaflets, posters and papers non-stop. Frank did visit her one day at the bookshop and spoke of the urgency of their work. 'Just one more push, that's all it might need, the unionists are on the run and the British are getting to know the score.'

As Sorcha arrived home one evening she saw the local priest leaving the house, and once inside she asked her ma what he had been visiting about.

'The church and some of the local business people want the barricades down,' her ma replied. 'They've been talking to that army major and he said the soldiers will guarantee our safety, but we're putting ourselves outside the pale if we keep the barricades in position.'

This raised a divisive discussion in the area, but the barricades were taken down a few days later much to the disgust of the few local republicans who had argued strongly against it. Sorcha had heard some people speak bitterly about the republicans' inability to produce guns for the defence of the area when they had been under attack. Indeed the words 'IRA = I ran away' had been painted on the gable end of a row of houses in the next street. There had also been rumours of arguments and splits within that secret organisation: it was said that those who were willing to fight were already preparing for another day.

On the TV news that night the newsreader said that the army, after three months in Northern Ireland, had started a hearts and minds campaign aimed at bringing the two communities closer together. The army hoped to restore confidence in its impartiality and good intentions. The news also said that in the United States of America Lieutenant William Calley was to be court-martialled on charges of murdering civilians at My Lai in Vietnam.

'Right chaps, you'll be pleased to hear we may get to see some action... against the paddies in Northern Ireland.' The second lieutenant looked at his assembled men and saw the surprise on some of their faces.

'Yes, they all said it would be a storm in a teacup, over in a few weeks. Well, seemingly that is all changing. So far our chaps haven't had much to do, except sit around and drink tea and be nice to everyone.' The lieutenant's voice took on a harsher tone. 'We've had reports that the natives are getting restless, they may need sorting out. Well, we're just the chaps to do that, eh.'

Over the weekend some of the squaddies heard Denis Healey, the minister of defence, say on the radio that some Rhine Army troops might be sent to Northern Ireland, but that these units would only serve four months at a time. The next week a notice on the company board stated that the unit would be undergoing riot training.

For Billy and his mates the new training brought a welcome relief from the usual barracks routine. They were issued with new equipment: riot batons, small steel shields and short-barrelled riot guns which fired CS gas canisters or the newly developed rubber bullets. The training was different and exciting too, as one half of the unit practised the formations and drills involved in using the new equipment, and the other half played the part of the mob. Dressed in their civvies, Billy and his friends liked to play the rioters, shouting abuse and throwing stones.

Once again it was the loyalist marching season, and once again the Unionist government was sanctioning provocative parades through nationalist areas. The people from Clonard watched resentfully as the orange marchers, led by flute bands, swaggered past up the Springfield Road. Between the marchers and the watchers stood a long line of British soldiers. There would have been no trouble, but for the taunts that the marchers hurled at the watchers as they came past the Mackies factory:

> If you're Irish come into the parlour,
> There's a welcome there for you.
> If your name is Timothy or Pat,
> You'll never get into Mackies,
> With a fenian name like that!

Some unemployed youths from Clonard, smarting under this insult and remembering Bombay Street which was now a bulldozed wasteland, began to throw stones at the marchers. The soldiers moved forward immediately to confront the stone-throwers, and a riot was only averted because the march had by now passed the area. But news travels fast in West Belfast and by the time the loyalist parade reached the edge of Ballymurphy, the nationalist people of that area were waiting for it and its army protectors.

A major battle ensued, with British soldiers moving into the estate in force, donning gas masks and saturating the area with CS gas. Confrontations occurred at every corner with sticks, stones and petrol bombs versus the soldiers' new arsenal of riot control equipment. That night the British general in charge of the troops appeared on TV to say that from now on his soldiers would shoot petrol-bombers dead.

People gathered on the streets in nationalist areas to discuss the situation.

'The Brits aren't up to much good, if they carry on like the RUC,' seemed to be the general opinion. This attitude hardened when the Unionist government let it be known that there would be no bans or restrictions on any of the loyalist parades to come. An official inquiry into the death of Samuel Devenny, who had been beaten up by the RUC in Derry the previous year, foundered when the detective from Scotland Yard met 'a conspiracy of silence' from the local police, and no action was taken. But Bernadette Devlin MP, who had been charged with riotous behaviour for her part in defending the Bogside, was sentenced to six months in jail.

The day after Bernadette was taken to Armagh to start her sentence, loyalist marches took place past various nationalist areas, including the isolated enclaves of Ardoyne in the northwest and the Short Strand across the river in East Belfast. Riots erupted as these parades passed by, and the British army refused to provide protection to these areas, which now came under siege from armed loyalist crowds who threatened to overwhelm them.

But out of the ashes of Bombay and many other nationalist streets that had been put to the torch, had emerged a reinvigorated republican organisation. The 'provisional IRA' seized the opportunity presented by the loyalist siege to prove that they now had the capacity to defend their areas. Gun battles took place in both Ardoyne and the Short Strand, to finish only when the loyalists were driven off. At the end six men lay dead, five attackers and one defender. The Provos had proved themselves, now the areas had their own defence force and would no longer have to rely on dubious friends from outside.

In the build-up to the main loyalist marches on the twelfth of July, tension filled the air. The loyalists, upset by the turn of events at Ardoyne and the Short Strand, howled for IRA blood. The Unionist government, backed by a newly elected Tory government in Britain, pledged they would bring 'law and order' to nationalist areas and rushed the Criminal Justice (Temporary Provisions) Bill through Stormont.

When Sorcha walked homewards that Friday evening, she was looking forward to the weekend. As she moved up the road towards the Falls she suddenly noticed that Albert Street was full of British soldiers and hurried by. She increased her pace again as she heard the sounds of a riot developing in Raglan Street and Balkan Street. Later, back in Clonard, Sorcha joined the groups of people gathering in the streets, who glanced now and again in the direction of the lower Falls. Amid the growls of heavy army vehicles, sporadic gunfire could be heard and a haze of CS gas rose into the air. Suddenly an army helicopter appeared in the distance above the rooftops, circling round and round, its loudspeakers proclaiming in a tinny voice, 'This area is now under curfew.'

Thousands of British troops converged on the lower Falls saturating the area and sealing it off. Then the searches started, with soldiers breaking into homes, wrecking them, and abusing the occupants.

Earlier on, just after Sorcha had passed by, a resident of the area, a disabled ex-serviceman who had spent ten years in the Royal Air Force, limped out onto the Falls Road with his hand raised to halt an army convoy. He wanted to warn the troops that the area was already hostile due to earlier raids, and that continuation could provoke an upsurge of violence. At the last instant he realised that the first army vehicle was not going to stop and he flung himself to one side. Instead of slowing, the Saracen deliberately accelerated, crushing him into the roadway. A passer-by who went to assist the fatally injured man was held back by two soldiers who thrust batons into his ribs and told him, 'Move on you Irish bastard, there are not enough of you dead.'

The curfew, although it was entirely illegal under the current law, carried on through the Saturday and into the Sunday, by which time the army had shot three more men dead. After the massive military presence achieved its dominance of the lower Falls, two open-backed army trucks slowly toured around the streets. Each vehicle carried a prominent Unionist politician and a pack of British journalists. Standing like Roman generals surveying a conquered province, the triumphant passengers were in turn peeped at, from behind net curtains, by the angry residents of the area.

Just outside the lower Falls, the people of Clonard continued to gather on the streets in an increasingly anxious state, animatedly discussing what could be done to help. British troops were everywhere around the perimeter of the curfew area, gas masks on and guns at the ready. The men shrugged their shoulders and shook their heads, 'There's too many Brits around to do anything,' they said.

'We could do something.' The speaker was a woman at the back of the crowd and people turned round to look at her.

'Us women I mean,' she continued hurriedly. 'They're choking their guts up with the gas, and they've got no food with the Brits keeping them in the houses – perhaps we could take some food in?'

People continued to stare at her and one man said scornfully, 'Don't be stupid, woman, the Brits would murder yous.'

The woman stood her ground. 'Not if there were lots of us, all together carrying food. We could walk right past them.'

The men still looked doubtful but Sorcha and the other women gathered round the speaker to discuss the idea. It had been agony standing about feeling helpless, unable to do anything, and the women decided to have a try to breach the curfew by carrying food in. They hurried around the areas outside the lower Falls, and just after midday hundreds and hundreds of women congregated behind Saint Paul's church in Cavendish Street each clutching bags of food and bottles of milk.

Sorcha's feelings had changed from apprehension to pride and exhilaration. She was marching with her ma and grandma, who had insisted on coming, saying nothing would stop them.

The solid ranks of women marched down the Falls passing through the cordon of soldiers as if they weren't there, then turned right down Leeson Street into the heart of the curfew area, distributing food as they went. The word passed quickly through West Belfast, and the women of Andersonstown, Turf Lodge, Ballymurphy and other areas hurried about determined to do their bit to help. At tea-time nearly three thousand women assembled at Casement Park, some with placards but all carrying provisions, and marched angry and determined on the British lines around the curfew area.

Once again the troops were nonplussed; some moved off, others stood to one side as the women passed straight through their lines and into the lower Falls. The influx of such numbers of women into the area made a mockery of the curfew and the search operation, so a decision was quickly made to abandon it.

The honeymoon period with the British army was at an end. Now the soldiers only appeared in force, clutching their weapons tightly, gazing backwards and forwards with quick turns of the head. Now there was no cup of tea, no greeting, just averted glances and muttered asides from the local people.

Women break the curfew

As the year passed there was still no word of a posting to Northern Ireland for Billy's unit. The soldiers felt left out, as other outfits based in West Germany had already completed tours. A rumour circulated that some of the London politicians thought the history of the unit might prove provocative if they were sent to that troubled province. The regiment's origins were in the seventeenth century, when it was raised as a militia to defend the Covenant, which was a Presbyterian statement of faith supported by many people throughout the lowlands of Scotland. The Covenanters, as they became known, suffered severe repression over many decades, till King William of Orange came to claim the British crown and established Protestantism as the official religion. The unit was then quickly incorporated into the crown forces, and served its new masters well in the years to come.

Some squaddies, upset by the thought that Westminster might be keeping them from an action posting, got a good laugh at the news that a CS gas canister had been flung into the House of Commons.

'I hear the fuckers were trying to climb over each other in their efforts to get out,' said Corporal Bruce. 'Serves them right, that'll teach them a lesson about the fenians.'

'Just be patient,' said Sergeant Wallace, who had been listening. 'They've had us in Korea, Malaya, Kenya, Cyprus and Aden, to name just a few in the last twenty years. At the moment they're still drinking tea with the paddies. When they want a few arses kicked, that's when they'll send for us.'

The sergeant smiled and quoted from his favourite poet, Kipling:

Oh it's Tommy this, and Tommy that
An' Tommy go away,
But it's thank you Mister Atkins
When the band begins to play.

'What's that racket?' Sorcha asked, jumping up and moving towards the window.

She was visiting her grandma, and the sudden clattering noise outside alarmed her.

'There's a raid on,' her grandma replied.

Sorcha turned back, 'A what?' she asked in surprise.

Grandma looked at her, 'A raid. Ach, I suppose it would have been long before your time. When the peelers came in force the women used to bang some pans together to make a racket, to warn the men, you see.'

Sorcha glanced at her grandma again, disbelief on her face, then moved quickly to the window. Sure enough across the street two young women were on their knees beating metal dustbin lids against the pavement. A third middle-aged woman was holding a tin bucket in one hand and striking it with the back of a scrubbing brush. Suddenly, above the racket the women were making, Sorcha could hear increasingly loudly the whine of heavy army vehicles. In a matter of minutes the streets were alive with troops, and a group of soldiers with riot batons in hand forced the women back inside their homes.

Sorcha stepped back when a passing bunch of soldiers leered in through the window at her. She was about to sit down with her grandma again when a thunderous knocking on the door made her jump. Sorcha looked at her grandma who was still sitting by the fire.

'Open up, in the name of the law,' bellowed a cockney voice, 'or we'll break the fucking door down.'

Sorcha looked at her grandma again.

'Better let them in,' grandma said.

Sorcha hurried to the door and opened it. Three soldiers burst past, pushing her against the wall in the process. Another soldier followed, holding a board with some papers clipped to it. This soldier, whom Sorcha took to be an officer, looked at the clipboard and asked for her granda. Sorcha tried to speak but no words came.

The officer looked at his list again. 'This is his house, isn't it?'

he asked.

'Yes, yes. I mean no. He's dead – he died five years ago,' Sorcha finally stuttered, just as one of the first three soldiers approached.

'Another good paddy, sir,' said the soldier, before asking the officer if they should search upstairs.

'Yes,' snapped the officer, flapping his arm as he waved the soldier away. Then he put his hand on Sorcha's arm and ushered her back into the living room where her grandma still sat at the fire-side.

'This is an arms search,' the officer said looking at Sorcha and then at her grandma. 'Acting on information received, we have reason to believe that arms may be hidden in this house.'

Loud crashes and bangs came from upstairs. Sorcha was rooted to the spot; she could not speak but glanced anxiously at her grandma, who sat unconcernedly looking at the fire.

The soldiers came back down the stairs and made for the front door. The officer looked in their direction as they came past the room. 'Anything?' he asked loudly.

The first soldier shook his head and continued out followed by the other two.

The officer turned to Sorcha. 'Well, frightfully sorry for the inconvenience, my dear,' he said, then followed his men out the door, closing it with a bang as he went.

Sorcha hurried round the rooms to see if any damage had been caused. In the kitchen the contents of the cupboards lay strewn all over the floor, but upstairs was the worst. Grandma's bedroom was wrecked with the bed upturned, the contents of the cupboard and chest of drawers scattered around, and the old fire-place ripped out from the wall.

Sorcha was near to crying as she ran downstairs to tell her grandma. As she blurted out about the damage the old lady looked up. Sorcha's voice dried up and she nearly choked: her gran was smiling fit to burst.

Grandma saw the look of horror on Sorcha's face. 'Five years, five years dead and gone, and the bastards are still chasing him,' she said chuckling away.

Sorcha had been about to burst into tears; instead as she looked at her gran she went into a fit of giggles. The tension left her body and she moved to sit on the arm of the old lady's chair, putting an arm round her.

Grandma looked up into Sorcha's eyes. 'Your granda would have had a great laugh about this, it'll make great crack when I catch up with him, bye and bye.'

They laughed together and Sorcha hugged her gran close.

When the area got over its initial shock, Clonard erupted. The women came out to harass the troops, while some of the youths fought running battles with the soldiers using stones and petrol bombs. The fighting continued sporadically through the night and into the next day, spreading to many of the surrounding areas. In the early hours of the fourth day of conflict, the provisional IRA killed a British soldier on the New Lodge Road, the first to be killed on active service in Northern Ireland for fifty years.

The unionist prime minister, Chichester–Clark, appeared on TV. 'We are now at war with the IRA provisionals,' he said, and the province braced itself as the streets rocked to the sound of gun battles and bombs.

It was raining as the soldiers unloaded themselves and their equipment onto the docks in Belfast. Rain swept down as they made their way in convoy through the streets. It's like Glasgow, but a lot smaller, thought Billy, as his eyes took in the passing scene. Glancing up he saw, half obscured by clouds, the hills in the background.

They made their way to the Springfield Road RUC barracks, which was to be their home for the next four months. The squaddies were in a sombre frame of mind; the tenth British soldier to die had just been killed, so the excitement of an action posting was tempered by the prospect of death or injury.

Before they had left Germany, the soldiers had been briefed about the situation by the officers who had spoken of agitators stirring up trouble and the menace of the IRA. The squaddies were also each issued with a booklet called 'Notes on Northern Ireland'. It set out a similar scenario to that of the officers, but also contained what was said to be the oath sworn by all members of Sinn Féin, the republicans' political organisation:

> 'I swear by Almighty God... by the Blessed
> Virgin Mary... by her tears and wailings... by
> the Blessed Rosary and Holy Beads... to fight
> until we die, wading in the fields of Red
> Gore of the Saxon Tyrants and Murderers of
> the Glorious Cause of Nationality, and if
> spared, to fight until there is not a single
> vestige and a space for a footpath left to
> tell that the Holy Soil of Ireland was
> trodden on by the Saxon Tyrants and the
> murderers, and moreover, when the
> English Protestant Robbers and Beasts in
> Ireland shall be driven into the sea like the
> swine that Jesus Christ caused to be
> drowned, we shall embark for, and take,
> England, root out every vestige of the
> accursed Blood of the Heretics, Adulterers
> and Murderers of Henry VIII and possess
> ourselves of the treasures of the Beasts
> that have so long kept our Beloved Isle of
> Saints... in bondage... and we shall not give
> up the conquest until we have our
> Holy Father complete ruler of the British
> Isles... so help me God.'

The young soldiers did not know that the oath was a complete forgery produced by unionist propagandists in 1918 as part of their campaign against Irish home rule. It had appeared regularly in loyalist publications ever since, but the oath bore no relation to reality whatsoever: Sinn Féin members did not take an oath of any kind.

Some of the squaddies were confused by the barrage of briefings, and asked Sergeant Wallace if he could explain things to them in simple terms.

He looked at the men and grinned. 'Look, the politicians will stand up in Parliament and say we're peace-keeping, the officers will say we're upholding the Queen's law and order, and we'll go in there and do a spot of paddy-bashing. That's what it'll come down to at the end of the day.'

Sergeant Wallace grinned at the soldiers again. 'Did I tell yous about the time I was in Singapore? Well there were these Yanks I met up with, they were on leave from Vietnam. They were just like us; their politicians went on about hearts and minds, so I asked them what that was all about. They laughed and said, "we've got a saying, man: if you've got them by the balls, their hearts and minds will follow."'

Sergeant Wallace and most of the men laughed loudly at the joke before the NCO continued, 'So don't you worry lads, we'll get by okay. A few micks don't represent much opposition.'

It took the soldiers some time to get used to their new surroundings. They were crammed into every available inch of space inside the RUC barracks and faced an increasingly hostile population outside. Billy's first visit to Clonard was with a search party looking for arms. At the briefing beforehand the officers had described the area as hardline. 'Full of terrorists, so watch out,' they had said.

When the officers had left, Sergeant Wallace grinned at the men. 'Don't worry lads, we're going in mob-handed, the micks won't know what's hit them. The motto is: do it to them before they have a chance to do it to you.'

The mass of soldiers moved into Clonard quickly in their armoured vehicles and sealed off the streets. Then the search parties went in, smashing down the doors if the residents did not respond immediately to the soldiers' knocking.

'We have it on good information that there is lots of terrorist material in these houses,' the officers had said.

'The micks are crafty bastards, so we'll leave no hiding place unturned,' said Sergeant Wallace.

This was the first taste of action for the soldiers, who swept into the task with enthusiasm. Wall units were torn out, carpets ripped up and floorboards lifted, beds and couches were overturned with covers slashed to search interiors. At the end the people were left to gaze in horror and anger at their wrecked homes, while the soldiers went out the way they had come, shouting in triumph to each other about arms finds and arrests.

The situation seemed to get more volatile by the day, as reports of bombings and shootings came in around the clock. The soldiers led a hectic life, out on patrol, rushing to riots, or spending hours on sentry duty waiting for danger to come to them.

Billy, with his section, was waiting to go out on patrol one day when a burst of gunfire at the front gate brought them running to the scene.

The gate sentry turned towards them. 'We were shot at, but I got the bastards,' he yelled excitedly, pointing across the road.

A van had mounted the pavement and smashed against the side of a house.

'Come on, let's get the fucking taigs,' snapped Corporal Bruce, sprinting out the gate and over to the van, followed by the rest of the unit. Corporal Bruce snatched open the right hand door; the driver fell out and sprawled on the roadway, blood staining the surface.

The soldiers looked at the body for a few seconds. 'This one's no good, he's kicked the bucket,' said Corporal Bruce, then reached into the van and pulled out the horrified passenger.

'Right, you bastard, you're coming with us,' snarled the corporal, dragging the terrified man across the road and into the barracks. Other soldiers offered willing hands to help the corporal, who, once the group was inside the gates, proceeded to batter at the man with his fists.

'Fire on us, you fucking taig,' screamed the corporal, as other soldiers joined in hitting the man, who fell to his knees under the blows. The soldiers started to kick the man, who desperately tried to protect himself with his arms.

'Stop! Stop!' At the urgent shouts the soldiers paused and looked round sheepishly.

The sergeant from the unit who had put out the sentries came running up.

'I think we've made a boob, lads,' the sergeant panted. 'I checked the van and the driver, but there's no sign of a gun. The other sentry thinks the van backfired.'

The soldiers looked at the sergeant in silence, till Corporal Bruce let out a laugh and prodded the man on the ground with the toe of his boot.

'You devious fenian fucker, trying to scare us to death with a backfiring van, what will they think of next?'

The sergeant looked at the soldiers for a minute, then his face broke into a grin. 'Better get him off to hospital,' he said, pointing to the man on the ground. 'Remember, he was injured in a traffic accident. There's not much we can do for his mate, he's snuffed it.'

Later on that evening the soldiers found themselves under siege inside the barracks, as a large crowd of local people surrounded the building, throwing stones, sticks and petrol bombs. The local IRA positioned a sniper on a rooftop opposite and added gunfire to the barrage.

'We're like the fucking US cavalry,' grinned Sergeant Wallace.

'Yea, and they're the Indians, big heap of fenian shit,' Corporal Bruce shouted back.

The soldiers felt fairly safe inside their fortified building, but later a soldier from another unit was shot dead in Ardoyne.

The squaddies stood around wiping the sleep out of their eyes.

'Right men, we leave in exactly ten minutes,' the lieutenant said. 'You should all try to reach your targets at roughly the same time.'

Corporal Bruce, Billy and five other soldiers had two addresses in the same street – both for known IRA terrorists, they were told at the briefing. At four in the morning the army vehicles eased their way out of the barracks and sped towards their destinations. The squaddies, feeling tense, gripped their weapons tightly: this opperation could end the troubles, they had been told. For some time the new unionist regime had wanted to bring in internment, and now the British Tory government had agreed.

'I'll knock the door, if it's not opened in thirty seconds – we break the fucker down,' Corporal Bruce gave out his last minute instructions in a loud voice. 'We go in quick, three go upstairs to search, and two stay downstairs. The rest give cover and help where required. When we get the bastards, we get out quick, into the lorry, then off before a crowd gathers.'

The screams of her ma jerked Sorcha awake. She had been vaguely aware of a thudding noise and shouting. Now she swept back the bedclothes and leapt to her feet. As she opened her bedroom door she came face to face with a soldier, his outstretched rifle pointing directly at her. Sorcha put her hand to her mouth to stifle a scream, then stepped back as the soldier kicked the door fully open and burst in.

The soldier's eyes flickered round the room. 'Are you the only one in here doll?' he asked, his eyes now gazing at her nightdress-clad figure.

Sorcha, not trusting herself to speak, nodded her head.

Just then another voice shouted out, 'We've got him!'

The soldier in Sorcha's room turned around, and she saw behind him two other Brits dragging her brother past her door and down the stairs. At the bottom of the stairs, Sorcha joined her ma, who was weeping and shrieking, trying to reach Seán to help him. Two soldiers pushed them roughly back as Seán was dragged out and thrust into the back of the army truck. At that moment an officer drove up in a landrover, and Sorcha's ma pleaded with him, 'You've got the wrong man, it's his da that would have been on your list.'

'What's his name?' snapped the officer to the soldiers.

'Seán Hoey, sir,' replied Corporal Bruce.

The officer looked at his list. 'That's the one we want,' he said.

'But that's his da's name too,' sobbed Sorcha's ma.

'Well, where is he then?' asked the officer, looking at his watch.

'Working away from home, but he only got on the list by mistake anyway.' Her ma broke into tears again as she answered, and Sorcha put an arm around her.

The officer flapped his hand at the soldiers by the truck. 'Right men, be off now,' he said, then turned back to Sorcha and her ma. 'We don't make up the lists, we only gather them up. I'll tell you what to do though. If his father is the one we really want, you send him round to the barracks, we might do a swop.' He grinned at the two women, then signalled to his driver and they roared off after the truck.

Sorcha kept her arm around her ma as they both slowly trudged back inside.

'He only had his trousers on,' her ma said. 'Not a shirt on his back, or shoes on his feet.'

The prisoners were taken to Girdwood Barracks to be processed for internment. The area was a hive of activity as army vehicles sped to and fro delivering prisoners then departing. Billy and another soldier took hold of Seán's arms as they hustled him out of the back of the truck and into a brightly lit gymnasium, where RUC and army intelligence personnel were processing the detainees.

Seán was pushed into joining a long line of prisoners, and

Billy with his mate stepped back to the edge of the room to take in the scene. As Billy glanced at the bustle around him he suddenly recognised a face that sent a shiver down his spine. He had noticed a man moving down the line of prisoners, who would now and again tap one on the shoulder as an indication to a second man, who then wrote something down on a clipboard he carried. Billy wasn't able to see the man's face till he got near the end of the line. The man stopped beside Seán, looked him over, then tapped him on the shoulder. At that instant Billy recognised him as the man who had supervised his own interrogation during the cadre course in Germany.

The next days were a nightmare for Sorcha and her ma. Try as they might they could not get any information out of the peelers or the army on the whereabouts of Seán or how he was. Snippets of information and rumour circulated in the nationalist areas: the men had been beaten and abused, some had been tortured. Spontaneous protests had erupted across the north and many people were killed or injured in clashes with the army or RUC. At her mother's insistence Sorcha continued to go to work.

'It'll keep you busy, and take your mind off things,' her ma had said.

As she made her way home, Sorcha remembered at the last minute about the medicine Teresa McCann had asked her to get for Gerry, and she hurried to the chemist's to buy it. When she got home, Sorcha popped into the McCanns' to deliver the medication and asked how Gerry was getting on.

'Ach, it's his chest still,' Teresa said, after thanking Sorcha for helping. 'The poor wee soul, he can't get his breath, but he always tries to do what the other kids do – play football and the like. Then he finds he can't get his breath and starts coughing, but it doesn't stop him, bless him, he just tries again.'

Sergeant Wallace had assembled the unit for the lieutenant to give a briefing.

'Well done, men. We've now got the troublemakers by the short and curlies, but we must keep that pressure up, then we might finish this once and for all. The powers-that-be want us to keep the buggers on the run, so we've been told to put ourselves about a bit, draw out the remaining gunmen. Then we can wrap up the situation before it gets out of hand.'

Sergeant Wallace and Corporal Bruce seemed delighted with this idea. 'We'll post a few snipers, and try to draw the terrorists out. We'll really stick the boot in,' they shouted, as they organised the patrols.

Later the landrovers swept out of the barracks and began slowly traversing the little streets. Billy's landrover screeched to a halt beside a couple of youths: the soldiers were under instructions to stop and search anyone found out of doors. 'And don't be too gentle doing it, either,' the sergeant had said.

The youths were pushed roughly against the wall of a house with arms and legs outstretched. One muttered a complaint about this treatment and received a rifle butt in the back for his pains.

As it began to get dark, Sergeant Wallace appeared in a landrover fitted with a microphone and loudspeakers. The sergeant was enjoying himself making up messages for the local population.

'Don't be vague, fuck over a taig.'

The sergeant scribbled something on the pad in front of him, then turned to look at the soldiers in the back. 'This should upset them,' he said, and picked up the microphone. 'We've interned all the men, now we're coming to fuck all the women,' the loudspeakers boomed.

The sergeant turned grinning to his men again, pointing a finger at Monroe as he did so. 'Except for Marilyn here, he'd do it the other way round,' he said, laughing loudly at his own joke.

Gerry McCann lay awake in bed, listening to the sounds of the soldiers and watching the headlights from the landrovers sporadically lighting up his bedroom through a gap in the curtains. He felt frightened and helpless: all the men seemed to have gone, and now the Brits were threatening the women. Suddenly a memory flashed into his mind. A few months ago, late at night like this, he had heard a noise and peeped out of the window. Two shadowy figures had been in the backyard of the house across the way. They had prised up a small manhole and inserted a bundle, then replaced the cover. Gerry remembered feeling a thrill: it must be some of the boys stashing arms, he had thought. He hadn't told anyone, not even his mum, and now an idea began to form in his mind.

He jumped out of bed and peered across at the yard again but there was no sign of movement: all the men were gone, arrested or off into hiding. As Gerry stood looking out the window, he suddenly heard Sergeant Wallace's message blasting out over the loudspeakers again. The women were being threatened: he felt desperate, then the idea became stronger in his mind. He, Gerry McCann, would defend the street. Sometimes they laughed at him when he tried to do things, but if he could get that gun he would show them.

Gerry hurriedly slipped on his clothes and crept silently downstairs. He went out the back, over the fence and into the yard of the empty house. He found a bit of metal to prise the manhole cover up and took out the sackcloth-wrapped bundle. Eagerly Gerry pulled at the covering, till suddenly the gun, a .45 Webley revolver, fell to the ground with a thud. As he picked it up, Gerry felt the grease the pistol had been coated in, and tried to clean it as best he could. Another small packet had fallen at the same time, and when he opened one end of it Gerry could see the bullets glinting dully. They were covered in grease also, but he inserted them awkwardly into the chamber just like he'd seen them do in the cowboy movies.

'Suspected gunman spotted in Cawnpore Street.' The wireless in Sergeant Wallace's landrover burst into life.

'That's Corporal Bruce, he's one of our snipers,' said the sergeant, turning to listen to the rest of the message.

He turned round again. 'He's seen someone with a revolver, but they disappeared before he got him in his sights. He wants us to try and draw him out again.'

Sergeant Wallace knew the area was saturated with soldiers so he ordered the driver to move slowly into the street and switched on the microphone, booming out his message again and again.

Gerry McCann was back inside his own house. Earlier he had moved out through the front door and looked around, but everything had been quiet so he'd moved back inside. Now he heard the soldiers coming again. Gerry gripped the pistol tightly and moved out the front door, then took up a position with his back to the wall and waited nervously for the soldiers to approach. Suddenly a crushing force to his chest thrust Gerry back against the wall. He looked around desperately to see who had struck him. There was no one, but he felt weak, he couldn't stand; his puzzled eyes looked upwards, then he pitched forward onto the street.

'I got the bastard!' The triumphant voice of Corporal Bruce crackled over the radio.

The soldiers, led by Sergeant Wallace's landrover, sped up the street to the McCann house and gathered round the body.

Billy prised the revolver from the boy's fingers and inspected it. 'Fuck me, it's covered in grease, it would never have fired in a million years,' he said, lifting the gun for them all to see.

Sergeant Wallace put the toe of his boot under the shoulder of the boy's body and jerked it over. Billy and the others gasped when they saw the face.

'It's only a bloody bairn,' said one, in a hushed whisper.

Sergeant Wallace looked at the soldiers. 'He may be only a kid, but he plays with dangerous toys,' he said.

A crowd had started to gather and the sergeant glanced at them. 'Right, get the stiff in the back of the landrover, then let's roll,' he said apprehensively. The lieutenant appeared just then. He took the microphone from the sergeant's vehicle and turned towards the crowd. 'Let this be a lesson to you. Any troublemakers will be interned, or shot if need be. My men don't care much which.'

Sorcha and her ma had visited the McCanns to try and take Teresa's mind off Gerry. Her husband was home now from the hospital, but he just sat by the fire, the top of his head covered in a white bandage.

'The doctors say he'll never be right again,' Sorcha remembered a neighbour saying, as he had tapped his head with a finger.

They were also desperately trying to find out about Seán. It was two weeks before their persistence bore fruit, and they learned he was being held in Crumlin Road jail. Three weeks later he was transferred, with many others, to the newly prepared camp at Long Kesh. Committees had quickly been formed in all the nationalist areas in support of the prisoners, with a minibus service to carry relatives to and from the camp.

That first visit to the Kesh, as it became known, was to remain a surreal image in Sorcha's mind for a long time to come. The corrugated iron topped with strands of barbed wire, the towers with the ever-watchful British soldiers: it was so like the prisoner-of-war movies set in Germany during the second world war.

Then there was Seán himself, with sunken eyes and hollow face, so unlike the brother Sorcha had known. He had clung onto them as they met, then sat down opposite clenching and unclenching his fists, till his ma put her hands gently over his. He hadn't wanted to talk about what had happened to him, he just said he was being kept in the hospital ward and that the doctors were kind and looked after him.

When his ma asked anxiously if he was all right, he looked away for a time before replying. 'Don't worry, ma, the doctors say there isn't a mark on me, sure I'll be right as rain again soon.'

After they arrived back home, Sorcha went out to fetch a bottle of milk. As she left the shop, she came face to face with the man who she had heard speaking to the shopkeeper about defending the area.

'Have you a minute love? I'd like a wee word with you,' he said, and Sorcha nodded her head.

'You've been up to the Kesh to see your Seán,' the man stated, and Sorcha nodded again.

'How was he?' the man asked, but did not wait for her reply. 'Not so good, eh?' His words were confirmed by the look on Sorcha's face.

'We think...' He started to speak again, then paused for a few seconds. 'Well, *some* people think that your Seán was one of the guineapigs.'

Sorcha gasped. She had heard this term used for a small group of internees who had been subjected to an intensive interrogation technique called sensory deprivation.

'The Brits have brought interrogators trained in Kenya and Aden into the North, to try their hand on our lads. Only we...' The man paused again, but this time did not correct himself. 'We know that most of the ones they did it on weren't ours.'

He put his hand on Sorcha's arm. 'The Brits may have done it as an experiment, like. Seán may take a while to get over it. Try and help him, and help your ma too, she's bound to have taken it bad.'

Sorcha's heart skipped a beat. No matter how many times I visit this place I'll never get used to it, she thought. One minute the minibus carrying the internees' relatives was travelling through a lovely countryside of green fields, the next you were facing the ugly corrugated iron walls, and towers festooned with layer upon layer of barbed wire. Her ma was feeling a bit under the weather, so Sorcha was making this visit on her own.

By now she had become used to the routine for visits: the waiting to be called, the searches before proceeding into the camp, and the scrutiny of the guards as you talked to your loved ones. Her brother was still in the hospital block, and Sorcha was agreeably surprised to find that Seán and herself would have that visiting room to themselves.

The soldier on guard looked older than the usual and seemed quite amiable. 'So you're young Seán's sister?' he said looking her up and down, then turned back to her brother. 'You never told me there was a beauty in the family.' The guard shook his head in mock reproach. Then, pulling a pack of cards from his pocket, he moved towards the table by the door. He grinned at Sorcha as he passed. 'If you get fed up talking to that brother of yours, you can come and play cards with me instead.'

Sorcha sat down at the table opposite Seán and pulled in her chair to get closer. He gave her a cheery smile, then indicated the guard who was by now playing patience on the table beside the door.

'That's Bobby, don't take any notice of what he says. He's not bad for one of them, he's got two months to go, then he's done his nine years. He's getting out then.'

Sorcha explained about their ma feeling unwell, but Seán surprised her by saying he was glad.

'Not because she's ill, or couldn't come,' he added hurriedly. 'But I need to tell someone what happened, get it off my chest like. I think that might help, I keep having nightmares about it.'

He explained that he thought it would upset their mother so he hadn't mentioned it before.

Sorcha leaned across and took Seán's hand. 'You can tell me,' she said softly.

Seán's face had a tormented look, but he attempted a smile,

then sighed and tightened his grip on Sorcha's hand.

'You and ma, yous saw me lifted. They shoved me into a truck, took me to a barracks and put me in a big room with a load more of our crowd. They were yelling and shouting at us, we had to get into lines. Then these two Brits, tough-looking bastards, came along picking odd ones out.'

Seán looked up from the table and paused for a minute. 'I was one they picked. When they got their full list we were taken away to another barracks somewhere. When we arrived they kicked us and beat us as we got off the lorry.'

Seán's voice faltered for a second. 'We had to pass through an avenue of Brits – they hit us, kicked us, battered us with anything they could lay their hands on. We were kept there for a day or two, I think. They wouldn't let us sleep, kept screaming and shouting at us.'

Seán hesitated. Imagining his pain, Sorcha felt tears rising, but fought them back. 'Go on,' she said.

Seán squeezed Sorcha's hand tightly. 'They came and hand-cuffed us, arms behind our backs. Then – they put these hoods over our heads. I nearly passed out, one of the others did, I think: you felt you couldn't breathe. Well, anyway, we were pushed and shoved out and we heard a great roaring noise, they said we were going for a trip in a helicopter. As I was pushed on board a Brit whispered in my ear that this was my first and last trip, that they would throw us out at twenty thousand feet. Well, we struggled after that, but with our hands cuffed...' Seán looked up and shrugged.

'There was a great roar and I could feel us rising, it was like being in a lift, except for the noise which was fierce. We felt like we'd been in the air for some time when a Brit shouts in my ear, "Right paddy, your time has come," and he shoved me towards the door. We were terrified and struggled to stay on, but we had no chance the state we were in. I – I thought it was my last moment, and when they pushed me off it seemed like hours, but I hit the deck almost straight away. They'd been playing with us, hovering a few feet off the ground. Then the Brits shoved us back on board, they were laughing, they thought it was a great joke.'

How could they do this, Sorcha thought. She was seething with hurt and anger, but struggled to control her emotions as Seán continued.

'Then the helicopter took off again and we went somewhere. I don't know where, but when we arrived we were pushed off and had to run the gauntlet again, even though we still had our hoods on and couldn't see. They hit me and battered me till someone led me into a building. They kept the hood on me, but took the rest of my clothes away. Someone had a look at me, I think it was a doctor; then they gave me a boiler suit to wear, it felt miles too big and sort of flopped around when I moved. The Brits came and grabbed me and took me off to some other room, made me stand with feet wide apart, leaning against a wall with my arms open and my fingers stretched out. There was this droning noise, like machinery – but high-pitched; it just went on and on, and they wouldn't let me move. They kept me against that wall for days and days, you just lost count.' Seán paused again and cleared his throat.

'It was so hot, very, very hot. The noise, it made your brain hurt, my arms and back began to ache. If I moved, the Brits were behind, they hit me on the hands, or kicked me in the back of my knees.' Seán's voice had reduced to a croak. 'Once – once I collapsed,' he said, then dropped his head and started to sob.

Sorcha tightened her grip on Seán's hand. Was this the civilisation the Brits were always saying they had brought to other countries, she asked herself. 'Perhaps you shouldn't talk about it any more. I don't mind if you can't go on,' she said quietly.

Seán looked up, choking back the tears. 'I must tell someone, don't you see? I must, I must,' he said fiercely.

He took a deep breath. 'Once I fell down – my mind went blank, I remember thinking I was floating, and I just collapsed. The Brits kicked me, dragged me up, then pushed me against the wall again. I had no food, I begged for water, the heat was awful, but they laughed and threw some water over my hood. I could hardly breathe, I felt like I was drowning. I... I...' Seán's voice dropped again.

'I had this dream, if you could call it that – a nightmare might be a better description. I felt I was floating, I just seemed to go out of myself.' He looked intently into Sorcha's eyes.

'I was floating, I was looking down, I was in this room like an operating theatre, like in a hospital, with bits of equipment here and there.' Seán paused.

'But the person doing the operation was like Frankenstein, he moved around jerky like. He was very big and he had a face like Paisley – it was Paisley and it was Frankenstein all rolled into one. In the corner was someone else, he looked like a top Brit, like Churchill, fat and dressed in tails and a bowtie and that. He kept telling the monster what to do, like it was a dog, saying, "good boy, well done." Then the Brit pointed the monster towards a figure I hadn't noticed before, lying on the operating table. I looked at the person on the table, he was all strapped down and couldn't move. I looked at the face to see who it was – it was me, I was looking at myself. I tried to warn myself, but I couldn't move. I could see but I couldn't move. The Brit was saying all they wanted was a few bits of me, that I wouldn't feel any pain. He said it would be good for me, make a better person of me, better than I was now. The monster got closer and closer, then I felt something in my mouth. I spat it out. It was put back in and I spat it out again.

'Then I felt a hand slapping my face, they weren't hitting me, just gently slapping me. I heard a voice saying, "I'm a doctor, I just want to take your temperature, this is a thermometer." I just broke down and cried. They gave me a cup of tea, it was hot and I tried to sip it but when the doctor had finished the Brits grabbed me and forced the hot tea down my throat. They dragged me off to another room and put the hood back on my head. They kept asking me questions. Who did I know in our area? Did I go on civil rights marches? Who did I know in the IRA? Did I know anyone who kept guns? They said all my friends were in the IRA and that I was too. I told them I didn't know, that I wasn't involved, but they kept on and on.'

Seán looked at Sorcha and shook his head. 'I don't know how long this went on, but I suddenly felt myself floating again. This time I woke with a crash as they threw me in a cell. They kept coming for me, dragging me off and asking questions: the same questions over and over again. The doctor came again, they took off my boiler suit and photographed me naked back and front. They gave me some food then and let me go to the toilet. They'd had me there just over a week, one told me, but it seemed like years.'

Seán's face had got more and more strained. But now he had spoken of his ordeal, he seemed to brighten up a bit. 'Then they sent me off to the Crumlin Road jail and gave me my clothes back, and told me I was interned.'

He stopped talking and they sat silently gazing at each other. Sorcha, struck dumb with pain and anger, conveyed her feelings of love and anguish through her face and eyes. She concentrated so intently that she did not hear the guard telling her the visiting time was up.

'I said "time up" darling,' the soldier muttered again, this time reaching out and shaking Sorcha by the shoulder. 'That was a cosy little chat yous had. I notice you didn't find time to come and play a round of cards with me.'

She looked at the guard uncomprehendingly before turning back to Seán and took both his hands in hers. Sorcha couldn't think of anything to say to comfort him, but squeezed his hands in hers, before leaving him sitting staring at the table top, as the guard ushered her out of the room.

On the way home in the minibus Sorcha sat silently gazing out the window thinking of Seán. Who were the people who could unleash the men who had done these terrible things to her brother? This was sophisticated torture and the practitioners must have been trained over a long period. Hadn't that republican said that the Brits had done this sort of thing in other places too? But who sanctioned it? Who made sure the torturers were trained and ready? And who gave the green light to go ahead?

The vehicle passed a couple of buildings, one with a union

jack fluttering from a makeshift flagpole, and a memory from the past came into her thoughts. She had been riding in a bus with her granda through Belfast. She'd only been little and had made some remark about the flag over the city hall, as it soared and fell in a stiff breeze.

'The butcher's apron, you mean,' her granda had replied, going on to explain that this was how many peoples throughout the world regarded the flag under whose shadow they were forced to live. Only now did she realise the significance of those words, and thought that from now on whenever she saw that flag it would remind her of Seán and his torture.

When Sorcha arrived home she sat down with her ma and composed an appeal to the authorities begging for Seán's release. Next day, at work, she typed the words out neatly and sent it off with a murmured prayer. She was deeply concerned by Seán's condition and the effect his ordeal might have on his future health. He needs lots of loving care and he will only get that at home, she thought.

Five weeks later, a few days before Christmas, Sorcha had given up hope of receiving a reply when she came home and found her ma sitting staring into the fire. Glancing up as Sorcha entered, her ma silently pointed to the official-looking envelope resting on the mantelpiece. Sorcha rushed across the room, picked up the letter and started to read:

'HM Government for Northern Ireland regrets
to inform you that it cannot recommend the
release of Sean Francis Hoey because from
August 1971 till the present day he has been
seen keeping company with known republicans.'

Sorcha exploded. 'But that's not fair, that's the time he's been inside. It's them that put him in there, how can he help the company he keeps?'

Her ma shrugged her shoulders resignedly. 'I know love, I know. But it's them that makes the rules, we're helpless. What can we do?'

Part Four

1972
Say hello to the Provos

And I say to my people's masters: Beware,
Beware of the thing that is coming, beware of
the risen people,
Who shall take what ye would not give...

Pádraic Pearse (The Rebel)

S orcha shifted to a more comfortable position in her seat. She
had been dozing for a while but now sat up and listened to
the discussion going on around her. They were all travelling
to Derry for the civil rights march, but as she listened Sorcha
sensed there was a definite edge to the banter being flung backwards and forwards on the bus.

'We have to keep building the marches. Non-violence is the
key, the British will have to listen in the end,' said one voice.

'The Brits will only listen when a few more of their crowd go
home in boxes,' cried another voice from the back.

Frank had been writing in a notebook, but now looked up
and smiled at Sorcha, then leaned across and stroked her arm. She
smiled back; he was more like his old self again, she thought. For
a while Frank had seemed depressed; she knew his final exams
were coming up later on in the year, but it had been the political
situation that was affecting him most. After internment, violence
had seemed endemic and civil rights activity had fallen away; but
now Frank was full of his old enthusiasm, talking about the build
up of marches and of the forthcoming one in Derry as the rebirth
of the movement.

The banter stopped for a few minutes as the crowd at the
front started to sing the civil rights anthem:

We shall overcome, we shall overcome,
We shall overcome some day.
Oh – deep in my heart, I do believe,
We shall overcome some day.

The whole bus had joined in the singing, including the crowd at the back, who now started up with a song of their own:

It all happened in seventy-one,
Internment it had just begun,
Men taken at the point of a gun.
Remember! We shall remember.

Put your faith in the Provos,
Put your faith in the brave.
Say hello to the Provos,
And Ireland will be saved.

At Bishops Fields, in Creggan, the assembly point for the march, the crowd just grew and grew. People felt elated with the turnout, but the atmosphere was tinged with apprehension. The authorities had not granted permission for the march; but then no civil rights march recently had received their assent. The people had marched anyway: after all these were their streets and they wanted justice.

As the demonstration made its way down the steep slopes to the Bogside, more people massed along the pavements, joining the march as they spotted friends in the throng. Frank guided Sorcha to near the front, intending to make sure they would not miss the speeches.

The crowd quickly swelled around the open-backed lorry that provided the platform at Free Derry corner. Tens of thousands were gathered, with more flooding in as Bernadette Devlin began speaking, introducing the first guest speaker, Fenner Brockway.

Suddenly shots were heard – unmistakably the distinctive crack of soldiers' SLRs – and three army Saracens sped past the high-rise flats with flashes appearing at their firing ports. Panic set in. Most people dropped to the ground at the first burst of firing, and now the loudspeakers on the lorry were screaming, 'Disperse! Disperse!'

People ran this way and that in desperate attempts to escape. Sorcha became separated from Frank in the confusion and found herself crammed, with a few others, behind a low wall. She was lying down trying to collect her thoughts when she became aware of a low moaning from the open space beyond the wall. As she peered towards the sound, she saw a man lying on his back some twenty yards away. Then a young fellow to her left eased himself over the wall and started crawling in the direction of the wounded man. The youth dragged himself halfway towards the man, but just then came a sharp crack and the young fellow rolled over screaming and holding his leg. Sorcha pushed herself up, intending to go to the youth's aid, when a soldier appeared on the open ground in front as if from nowhere. He stopped about twenty yards short of the screaming figure, knelt on one knee, slowly raised his rifle to his shoulder and fired a shot into the youth's body.

Later Sorcha found herself standing with other shocked people at the entrance to a small shop on the edge of the Bogside. The shopkeeper telephoned the hospital for details of the casualties and they all stood silent, with open mouths and hearts pumping, as the man slowly wrote out the long list of dead. Afterwards, back in Belfast, she kept remembering the killing she had witnessed. The soldier, after shooting the youth, had turned towards another group of soldiers Sorcha could not see and made a thumbs up gesture. She had heard them though. 'Congratulations,' they had shouted, then burst into song:

You've just been shot by the armee-e,
Doo-da, doo-da,
You've just been shot by the armee-e,
Doo-da, doo-da, day.

Billy moved cautiously down the street, taking short tight steps and moving his head from side to side, as he strained every nerve waiting for the inevitable to happen. Suddenly, behind him across the street, a door crashed open. Billy turned quickly, the SLR fitting automatically into his shoulder as his eyes took in the figure framed in the doorway. He saw what he took to be a weapon in their hands and squeezed the trigger of his rifle.

'Congratulations, lance corporal,' sang out the sarcastic voice of the officer over the tannoy. 'I can just see the headlines in the Irish News: "Bridget O'Reilly, mother of ten, shot by British soldier."'

Billy blushed as the WRAC in the doorway opposite, clutching a broom, giggled back at him.

'All right, continue,' rang out the officer's voice from the control tower again. 'At least your shooting was spot on, lance corporal. She wouldn't have raised any more Irish brats.'

Billy turned to continue, making his way stealthily down the street past the Shamrock Bar and O'Hara's hardware store. Well, at least he had survived his first Northern Ireland tour, Billy thought, and now back in Germany the soldiers had a realistic environment in which to practise their patrolling techniques and get the feel for the ever-increasing armoury of riot control equipment. Tin City was a complete reconstruction of an Irish street, just like the frontier towns in Western movies, built in a training area close to their barracks.

The soldiers had the most fun with the baton gun which fired a six-inch-long piece of hard black rubber with a rounded nose. An officer had found some dummies which a German clothes shop had thrown out, and these were used as targets. The guns were not very accurate so the soldiers often missed their targets, but when they registered a hit, the dummy was sent flying through the air to a chorus of cheers.

Sergeant Wallace told the men laughingly that they were actually doing the Irish a favour when they fired rubber bullets.

'We've locked up their men, see, so the ladies are a bit short of pleasure. So if we fire a few of them, then the fenian bitches can pick them up for comfort through the night. I'm sure one of these,' he held up the rubber bullet, 'will give them a better fuck than they ever got from those weeds they call men over there.'

Later, back in the barracks, Corporal Bruce showed some of the soldiers how bits of razor blades could be fitted into the nose of the bullets, and how batteries, of the same diameter, could be slipped down the gun barrel to be fired in front of the round.

The arrival of a new soldier from training camp caused some consternation in the barracks, because although he spoke with a strong Glasgow accent the new soldier was black. On parade that first morning, Sergeant Wallace, reading out the roll call, slowed as he came to the new name.

'Robertson, Patrick Lloyd,' he called out.

The new man came smartly to attention. 'Here sergeant!' he cried.

The sergeant walked slowly over to him. 'Patrick, eh. I hope you're not a fucking paddy?' he asked.

The new man shook his head. 'No sergeant.'

Sergeant Wallace looked at his list of names again. 'Robertson, eh. Any relation to the jam people?'

Again the new man shook his head, and the sergeant gave him a long look before saying, 'No? You look awfie like their mascot to me.'

The sergeant turned chuckling towards the rest of the men. 'He looks *golly* well like it, eh, lads,' he said, and most of the soldiers grinned back.

Afterwards the newcomer was called Golly by most of the other squaddies and in the end had to resignedly accept it as his nickname.

Sergeant Wallace did not regard himself as prejudiced, but felt that if blacks came into the army then it was better for all concerned if they knew their place. Discipline with a strong hand to guide them would therefore be beneficial, not least to themselves.

The sergeant resolved to provide just such guidance for the new soldier should the need arise. In fact the need did not arise very often as Robertson threw himself into all aspects of army life with an enthusiasm and effort that left many others trailing in his wake. He had learnt early that blacks had to be out in front before they had any chance of being regarded as equal.

But Sergeant Wallace was a patient man who could wait his opportunity. He thought of himself as cultured and prided himself in the poetry that he made up. Sometimes he would make a defaulter stand to attention and repeat one of his ditties. Sergeant Wallace had made up some verses for Robertson, but it was some time before he found an opportunity to make use of them.

One day it was reported to him that 'Golly' had given backchat to Corporal Bruce. The fact that the corporal was continually trying to bait the black soldier was not taken into account. Before giving Robertson some extra duties as punishment, Sergeant Wallace gave him a lecture about the dangers of getting a chip on his shoulder. Then he made him stand to attention and chant aloud the sergeant's ditty:

> Black might be beautiful,
> And Brown may be grand,
> But White is the colour
> Of the Big Boss Man.

Another newcomer to the unit received a different reception from Sergeant Wallace. Willie Muir was a farmer's son, and the sergeant liked nothing better than shooting a bit of game when on leave. The sergeant mentioned this to the new soldier, and it was arranged that on their next leave he would visit the farm, bringing his twelve-bore shotgun with him, to indulge in his favourite recreation. In return the sergeant took Muir under his wing. The newcomer was a bit slow at most things, but he was a good shot and the sergeant encouraged him to get better. The new soldier got marksman scores at the unit-firing on the ranges, and on the recommendation of Sergeant Wallace was made one of the unit snipers and given a rifle with telescopic sights. On leave before his first Northern Ireland tour Willie Muir practised nearly all the time, shooting rabbits and hares with his dad's .22 rifle.

Billy went on leave back to his native Glasgow, and proudly showed his ma and da the stripe sewn on the arm of his uniform.

'First step up the ladder, eh,' his dad said, and his ma held up the sleeve of the jacket and looked at the v-shaped stripe. Billy felt apprehensive because, when the leave was over, another tour of Belfast beckoned. Things were hotting up there and the toll of dead soldiers was mounting. Still, there was the leave first and as the sergeant said, 'Weren't they just the boys to quieten things down again.'

Billy was finding it more difficult to meet his old mates as some were now married or had moved on. He still found one or two in the pubs they used to drink in, but even then they seemed to have less in common now than before. Some of his army mates had suggested visiting each other's places on leave. Up till now Billy had resisted this, but now he felt that next time it might be a good idea as he found himself increasingly on his own.

At least there was the match to go to: he was lucky as his leave coincided with an old firm match, with Rangers this time the visitors to Parkhead. Billy found himself on the terraces at the Rangers end, engulfed in a sea of fans waving their red, white and blue banners and scarves, and shaking their fists at the Irish tricolour flying over the stadium.

The game itself was a dour affair with Celtic's attacking thrusts, led by wee Jimmy Johnstone and Kenny Dalglish, foundering on the big resolute Rangers defenders marshalled by John Greig. As the match on the pitch fizzled out, the verbal battle on the terraces began to hot up. Both sides exhausted their repertoire of traditional songs and started to bring in the newer ones. The Rangers fans started with their song about the army shootings in Derry:

Bang, Bang, Bang, Bloody Sunday,
Hey, Hey, Hey, what a beautiful day.

Then they launched into their version of Lee Marvin's

'Wandering Star':

> I was born under a Union Jack,
> I was born under a Union Jack.
> If guns are made for shooting,
> Then skulls are made to crack.
> You've never seen a better Taig,
> Than with a bullet in his back.

Until now the Rangers crowd had been making so much noise that Billy could not hear any of the Celtic songs. Now there was a lull in the voices from his side of the terraces, and he listened as the Celtic fans replied with verses that filled him with dread and rage:

> The IRA shot a British soldier today,
> A British soldier today,
> A British soldier today-ay-ay-ay.
> The IRA shot a British soldier today,
> And they'll shoot another one tomorrow.
>
> So we say support the IRA,
> Support the IRA,
> Support the IRA-A-A-A.
> We say support the IRA,
> And we'll have a United Ireland tomorrow.

As the game petered out into a goalless draw, fighting broke out on the terraces and continued haphazardly into the streets outside. Next day the papers described the match as relatively trouble-free, with only sixty-four arrests made by the police.

Dawn was lighting up the sky and a gentle rain started to fall, as the ferry carrying the soldiers moved towards the dock through Belfast lough. Billy joined a group of squaddies standing on the deck, silently watching the approaching city. A soldier quietly began to sing the Rangers fans' version of 'Nobody's Child':

As I was slowly passing a Catholic church one day,
I stopped just for a little while to hear the Fenians pray.
Alone a priest was standing and when I asked him why,
He looked at me with eyes that could not see,
And he began to cry.

Billy and the other soldiers now joined in with the tune changing to that of the 'Red Flag':

Hello, hello, how do you do,
We are the boys in royal blue.
We are the boys who'll do or die,
To keep the red-white-an'-blue flag flying high.

The men were issued with ammunition for their weapons, and were met as they docked by soldiers of the outgoing unit, who supplied lorries and landrovers to take them to their new billets. This tour of duty was to cover the same area as last time, but a barracks had now been constructed in an old mill off the Falls Road with a high wall of corrugated iron built around it.

The men took up defensive positions on the vehicles and moved off through the rain towards their new home. Sergeant Wallace had Willie Muir travelling in the back of his landrover, clutching the sniper's rifle, with Billy and Monroe riding shotgun, standing at the back.

Billy watched the sullen-looking faces of the people of the Falls as the landrover sped past them. Then the convoy slowed as one by one the vehicles entered through the gates of the new fortress. Suddenly Billy heard a sharp crack and felt the wind of a bullet passing his right ear. Pandemonium broke out as the convoy jerked to a halt, and the sentry at the gate started firing at the window of a house opposite. Billy joined the other soldiers frantically scrambling behind the now stationary vehicles to get into cover. In a few minutes things calmed down a bit; no more shots had been fired at the soldiers, and now the men looked around to see if anyone had been hit. They did not appear to have suffered any casualties, but then Sergeant Wallace turned to Billy.

'Where's Willie Muir?' he asked.

They looked at one another for a second, then both dashed to the back of the landrover. Willie Muir lay in a pool of blood, his hands still cradling the sniper's rifle.

Sorcha looked around warily as she left home on her way to work. She was thinking about the conversation she had overheard in the shop last evening. As she had joined the queue someone had said that a new British army unit had come into the area.

'They're them Scotch bastards,' said the woman in front of Sorcha.

'They're the ones that killed Teresa McCann's wee lad,' said another voice.

'Aye, well, they lost one of theirs this time – before they got in the gate even, or so I hear,' said the man behind the counter.

As Sorcha made her way along the Antrim Road towards the bookshop she noticed a man, with two women, unlocking the door of the Gemini Health Studio. This was a new business which advertised 'attractive masseuses' in the local papers. Later in the day Victor was fixing a broken bookshelf when he suddenly stopped, put a hand to his ear and called out to Sorcha, 'What's that? Did you hear?'

She stopped sorting out a box of books and, listening hard, heard a sound like gunfire. She made her way to the door and looked out. 'Sounded like shooting, but it looks all quiet out there now,' she said, stepping back inside.

All was quiet for a few more seconds, then the roar of a car engine and the screeching of tyres filled the street. Sorcha, followed this time by Victor, hurried back to the door but the street was now empty of traffic. Other people were looking out of windows or standing outside doors, including a group of excited-looking women in low-cut dresses outside the Gemini Health Studio.

All was quiet for about ten minutes, then the street vibrated to the sound of sirens as the RUC, army and two ambulances rushed along and screeched to a halt outside the massage parlour. Soon the area was saturated by peelers and soldiers who ordered all onlookers back inside their shops and buildings. The radio carried no news of any incident in the road, but was reporting a shooting on the Twinbrook Estate in West Belfast where a laundry van had been caught up in a gun battle.

The road was still packed with troops and police as Sorcha left to go home that evening. Later, walking back into Clonard, she paused for a minute to listen to a group of men talking excitedly on a street corner. One of them was saying that the word was that 'the 'RA had wiped out a few Brits' engaged in some sort of undercover work.

When she went back to work the next day, Sorcha was still puzzling over the previous day's events. Soldiers and peelers were still out in force along the road, and the windows of the Gemini Health Studio had been boarded over.

The bookshop had been open about an hour, when an RUC man came in to ask Sorcha and Victor questions about what they had seen or heard yesterday. Before he left, the peeler requested their names and addresses which he wrote down carefully in his notebook. At about three in the afternoon there was a sudden screech of brakes and the bookshop door burst open as three soldiers and two peelers rushed in, followed by an officer. Sorcha and Victor were made to stand against one wall, watched by a soldier with pointed rifle, while behind them the bookshop was ransacked.

The officer then began to question Sorcha about where she lived and who she knew in the area. After answering a few of the officer's questions, she timidly asked in return, 'What is this all about?'

The officer stared at her for a few moments before answering.

'Someone's been supplying information to the IRA about the place down the road. We think it might be you.'

Sorcha felt her heart beat faster and for a few seconds could not trust herself to speak. Then she cried out that she did not even know what had happened. The officer seemed to disbelieve her cries of innocence and ordered the soldiers to take her in for further questioning.

As two soldiers grabbed Sorcha's arms and hustled her towards the door, Victor attempted to intervene. One of the soldiers swung round. 'Fuck off, Yid,' he snarled.

A peeler pulled Victor roughly from behind. 'Behave yourself, Jew boy, or we'll have another search and this time we'll wreck the fucking gaff,' he said.

Victor could only watch helplessly as she was dragged out of the shop and pushed into the back of a landrover which roared off up the road. Sorcha's mind was in turmoil: one minute she had been thinking that in a short time she would be going home, and the next she was a prisoner in the back of an army landrover going god knows where.

The speed of the vehicle slackened as the driver negotiated the gateway to a barracks and drove inside. Sorcha kept telling herself to remain calm as the landrover jerked to a halt and the soldiers hustled her out and into a building. All her belongings were taken off her before she was forced down a passageway and into a bare white-walled room, with a table and two chairs in the centre. The escorting soldier told Sorcha to sit on one of the chairs while he stood back against the wall watching her.

Some time passed and Sorcha was screwing up her courage to ask the soldier what would happen now, when the door burst open and two other soldiers entered. One had close-cropped dark hair and carried a police baton, which he kept thudding against the open palm of his other hand. The second man had longer fair hair; he smiled at Sorcha, then motioned to the soldier who had been on guard that he could go. The dark-haired man stood close to Sorcha, glaring down at her and still hitting the palm of his hand with the baton. Feeling intimidated, she looked away, and the man immediately swung the baton down, striking the table with a loud crack. Sorcha jumped in alarm and the man laughed, then bent over, screwing up his face and thrusting it close to hers.

'I'm fed up with you fucking fenians,' he snarled. 'Our blokes get the chop and none of the paddies knows fuck all about it. Well, we'll see about that, eh.'

In the meantime the fair-haired man had sat on the seat opposite Sorcha. With a muttered curse the dark-haired man waved the baton inches from her face. Then he turned on his heels and moved to the small window at the back of the room where he stood looking out through the bars.

The fair-haired man leant forward confidently, smiled at Sorcha and whispered, 'Sorry about him, he's upset; some of his friends were killed in that shooting, near where you work. It'll be best if you tell us all you know – we don't want to upset him again, do we?'

Sorcha explained that she had already told all she had heard and seen, but the fair-haired man smiled once more and started to go over the questions again and again. After what seemed to be ages of consistent probing, he started to ask about her brother Seán, inferring that he was an IRA man and that she was also helping that organisation.

Sorcha felt that she could take no more, even if the man appeared to be friendly. 'That's all I'm saying, this is just going round in circles. I've told you all I know,' she snapped.

The fair-haired man smiled again at her and coughed loudly. The dark-haired man spun around from the window and marched purposefully towards Sorcha, thudding the baton into the palm of his hand as he did so. He stopped inches from her and thrust the baton under her chin, forcing her head up.

'I'm getting fed up with this,' he snarled into her face. 'You'd better start coming up with some answers or you're in trouble, little girl.'

He looked across at the other interrogator. 'I bet she's an IRA groupy – look at her mouth, I bet she does lovely blow jobs.'

The man looked back into Sorcha's face, keeping the baton under her chin. 'Do you suck IRA cocks?' he sneered.

She jerked her head away in disgust, and the dark-haired man brought the baton thudding down on the table again. Sorcha remembered Seán telling her about his interrogation. She took a deep breath and steeled herself: I won't answer any more questions, she thought. She fixed her eyes on a spot on the wall and stared at it, only stopping when the dark-haired man angrily jerked her head around.

The night seemed to pass in a haze, with persistent questioning from the fair-haired man interspersed with obscenities shouted into her face by the baton-carrier. Sorcha concentrated on the spot on the wall, and thought of things that had happened in the past. She remembered vividly the visit to Cave Hill with her gran and granda and what had been said about the United men.

Suddenly the two interrogators looked at each other, then left the room, the dark-haired one thudding his baton onto the table one last time before he disappeared. The guard soldier re-entered and escorted Sorcha to a small cell which he thrust her into, locking the door with a slam.

Later on that morning Sorcha was released, and as a soldier pushed her out of the barracks gate she was surprised to see her ma and another woman standing outside waiting for her. She rushed over to hug her ma, who introduced the woman as Eileen, and explained that she had helped by ringing around all the barracks and RUC stations till this one had admitted holding her.

Back home the tired but happy women sat drinking a welcome cup of tea, when a sudden thought came into Sorcha's mind.

'But how did you know I'd been lifted in the first place?' she asked.

Her ma smiled. 'It was that fellow you work for, Victor isn't it? He came walking up the road asking for Sorcha's mother, and a wee lad brought him round here.'

Sorcha had forgotten all about Victor, and immediately felt concerned. 'Was he okay?' she asked. 'He gets a bit shaky sometimes.'

'He appeared a bit shocked,' answered her ma, 'but he insisted on telling us everything that had happened. I gave him a cup of tea, and I got the shop to call him a taxi to get him home again.'

After a meal and freshening up, Sorcha, although very tired, insisted on going back to the bookshop. 'I want to thank Victor, and check he's all right,' she said.

As she entered the bookshop Sorcha was surprised to see no attempt had been made to clear up after the soldiers' and peelers' search. At the sound of the shop bell, Victor appeared from the back. Sorcha ran over to him and threw her arms around him, thanking him for going to her ma.

He embarrassedly shrugged off her thanks. 'Anyone would have done it,' he said.

Victor seemed in a rather pensive mood, and Sorcha laughingly suggested that he seemed to be taking it harder than herself.

Victor stared at her for a minute, then bit his lip and looked at the floor. 'I... I'm going to sell up,' he said. 'Sell the shop – leave. I'm getting out.'

Sorcha looked aghast, then her anger rose. 'What's happened here wasn't very nice, but it happens all the time in Clonard. I told you about Seán, what he went through – it's us that's getting hit, you probably won't get troubled again.'

Victor stood silently for a little while, then went over to the record player in the corner, on which he sometimes played one of the classical LPs that he got at house clearances from time to time. Now he put on a single, and Sorcha was surprised to hear the gravelly voice of Louis Armstrong singing 'Mac the Knife':

Oh the shark has pretty teeth, dear,
And he shows them pearly white.

Victor turned to Sorcha. 'That song was written by Bertolt Brecht. He was the same as me – a German Jew. He wrote it about the coming of fascism – the Nazis. He managed to get out – before – before...' Victor choked for a few seconds then recovered. 'We – me and my family – we did not get out.'

Victor slowly rolled up his shirt sleeve to show a faded number roughly tattooed on his arm. 'I also had the early morning knock on the door. I did survive – my family did not.' His voice cracked over the last sentence and his head slipped down.

Sorcha silently went to Victor and hugged him close.

'I'm all right now,' he said after a couple of minutes. He stepped back and moved to the record player, which was now grinding at the end of the record, and switched it off.

Victor turned again to Sorcha. 'You see, my happiness now, it depends on me forgetting,' he said, gesturing with his hand. 'What's happening here, now, yesterday, tomorrow – it will not stop now. It reminds me, it's too painful.'

A long silence followed.

'I understand. I'm sorry, I didn't know,' said Sorcha softly, then asked, 'But where will you go?'

Victor smiled at her fondly. 'We're a people who have got used to travelling,' he said. 'Across the water perhaps. I have friends in Leeds, I may go there.'

Victor had made up his mind. Within a month the stock of books had gone and the shop had been sold. On the last day Sorcha and Victor sadly shook hands as they said goodbye.

'I'm sorry this has happened, you've lost your job,' said Victor.

Sorcha smiled back. 'Don't worry about me, I'll be okay. I hope you'll remember some good things about us,' she said.

'I'll always remember the people and the place. I would have stayed if it hadn't been...' He hesitated, then shrugged his shoulders. 'But most of all I'll remember you,' he continued, as they hugged and said goodbye.

A few days later Sorcha bumped into the man from the end of the street again.

'I hear you're out of work,' he said, nodding his head in welcome.

'Yes,' she said, then asked if he knew what was behind the incident on the Antrim Road.

'It was to do with this top Brit they've put in charge of Belfast – yer man was in Kenya and Malaya, he's obsessed with intelligence and information gathering.'

He looked around. 'Well, some of the boys found out that the

Brits were running this laundry service. They did a good job too from what I hear – cleaning the clothes I mean. But the Brits were running it, they had spy holes in the top of the van and all the clothes were forensically tested before they were cleaned.'

The man looked around again. 'The Antrim Road job was part of that type of thing. The Brits were running this massage parlour – you know the sort of things that go on in them places...' He looked embarrassed. 'Well, the Brits were taking photos of the clients, two-way mirrors and that, and threatening to send the pictures to their wives or family – unless they agreed to spy for them. It wasn't just our crowd they did it on, the orangies got the same treatment on that one.'

He touched Sorcha's arm. 'The Brits had you in, so I hear.'

Sorcha nodded, then told him about working in the book-shop and being taken into the barracks. She finished by telling him about the shop closing and he looked at her sympathetically.

'I'm sorry yous got dragged into it. But something had to be done, so the lads smashed them up, the laundry and the massage parlour at the same time, and sent a few Brits home for their tea.'

The man turned as if to go, then faced Sorcha again. 'You looking for another job?' he asked.

Sorcha nodded her head eagerly.

'Well, it's not much,' he said. 'But the club is looking for a cleaner, so I hear. It won't pay a lot, but it might tide you over. I'll put a word in for you if you like.'

Billy tightened the straps on his webbing and looked at his black-ened face in the mirror. They were about to go out on night patrol. The soldiers had just spent the last fortnight on lookout duties in an observation post on the roof of the old mill. The boredom had been intense, watching the street hoping to recog-nise a 'wanted' face, or just jotting down sightings of certain indi-viduals or movements around specific locations. The nights hadn't been a lot better, but at least they could sometimes amuse themselves by using the night glasses to peep into the windows of nearby houses, and, if they were lucky, catch one of the local women undressing.

Their fortress had been hastily constructed, and the accommodation for the soldiers was sparse and cluttered. Bunk beds were the norm, with as many squaddies as possible crammed into a room. Off duty, men could do little but drink and sleep. Pin-ups were plastered over the walls with the soldiers adding their own messages to some of the more suggestive pictures.

'Right men, get fell in outside,' yelled Corporal Bruce.

They were inspected in turn; equipment, especially, was given the once over. They were then issued with ammo, rubber bullets and rounds of CS gas for their night's work.

Billy went to the big concrete block at the gate and took up a covering position, and suddenly the rest of the patrol burst out past him, spreading out to take up positions across the road.

Sorcha was feeling pleased: she had persuaded her ma to come out for a change. It'll do her good, she thought, as she exchanged

PHILIP JONES-GRIFFITHS/MAGNUM

some banter with the man behind the bar while she bought a round of drinks. Since she had got the job as a cleaner, Sorcha had started to visit the club from time to time. It was run by republicans, mainly ex-prisoners, and any proceeds went towards the needs of prisoners and their families. Sorcha found a table for her ma and herself, and they were soon joined by others from the area whom they knew.

The group Saoirse – Freedom – started off the evening with a selection of republican songs, and then the comedian Wee T. Haig took over.

'A funny thing happened in the club tonight,' he started. 'I heard a wee woman standing up for the Brits.'

There were cries of derision from the audience.

'It's true, it's true,' he shouted back. 'There was this group of women and they were saying that British soldiers weren't fit to live with pigs... All except this one woman, she stuck up for the Brits and said they were.'

After the laughter, he continued, 'Did yous see the peelers in the area today? Three peelers and a hundred Brits – normal policing, of course.' The comedian paused.

'Have yous noticed how the peelers always appear in threes? Do yous know why? Well, one can read, one can write and the third keeps an eye on the two intellectuals.'

Wee T. took a sip from his beer glass.

'I was in the city centre the other day, you know what it's like: dodging the Brits and the peelers, hoping they won't stop you and ask where you're from.' He made a cutting motion across his throat.

'Well, there I was, and suddenly this lady pops out and stops me. She had this little clipboard with some sort of form on it – would you credit it, a poll of attitudes to the situation. Did I support a united Ireland? I looked around, up and down. Who commissioned this poll, love, I said. It wasn't the Brits or the UDA? Then came the sixty-four-thousand dollar question – what do you think of the bright new shiny Ulster Defence Regiment?'

Wee T. took another sip of his beer. 'What would you have

Off duty

said in the middle of Grand Parade? Well, I said, let me tell you a parable, love – you know how the Brits think we've got religion coming out our ears. It's the parable of the rich American and his three sons. He was so rich, oil wells and that, he didn't know what to do with his money. But he had three sons and the eldest was coming up for twenty-one, so he thought, I know what I'll do, I'll give my three sons anything they want. So he asked the eldest one what he would like. "Oh, I like oil wells, dad", said he. "I want some of my own." "No problem, son," said the father, and he flew to London and bought him British Petroleum. The next son was fifteen, and when his dad asked him, he said, "Oh dad, I like airplanes, dad, I'd love some of my own." "No problem, son," said the da, and he flew to London and bought him British Airways. Now your man's third son was only six years old, so his dad knelt down to ask him to name anything he wanted. The boy thought for a minute, then he looked at his da and said, "The only thing I really, really want – is a cowboy outfit." "No problem, son," said the da, and he flew to London and bought his boy the UDR.'

The group, Saoirse, had come on again when the whisper went around that a Brit patrol was in the area and might enter the club as they frequently did. The group started up with their next song, 'My Little Armalite':

> I was stopped by a soldier, said he, 'you are a swine,'
> He beat me with his baton and kicked me in the groin,
> I bowed and I scraped, sure me manners were polite,
> But all the time I'm thinking of me little Armalite.

> And it's down in Clonard, that's where I long to be,
> Lying in the dark with a Provo company,
> A comrade on me left, and another one on me right,
> And a clip of ammunition for me little Armalite.

Billy and the rest of the patrol burst into the club and moved around in threes staring at the seated groups of locals, now and again asking for names and addresses. Corporal Bruce started to question a crowd of young men near the stage, and the other soldiers gave Saoirse hostile looks as they completed their second set for the night.

Wee T. Haig hurried forward clutching a little ukulele in one hand and grabbed the microphone with the other. 'This is a special request for our friends from across the sea, the poor souls are homesick, so they are. So I'll give them a George Formby number, just to make them feel at home.'

He started to strum the ukulele vigorously and launched into a mock Lancastrian accent:

> I'm leaning on the lampost
> At the corner of the street,
> I'm waiting for a certain little soldier to come by,
> Oh me, Oh my,
> A certain little soldier to come by.

The tension in the air deepened: many soldiers had been killed or injured in street ambushes already that year. Suddenly an argument broke out between Corporal Bruce and the young men he had been questioning. A glass of beer was thrown over one of the soldiers and the thrower received a rifle butt in his face. Immediately there was uproar, with running battles between the soldiers and groups of locals; glasses and bottles flew while the soldiers used their batons and rubber bullet guns.

On an order from Corporal Bruce, the soldiers retreated to the door. The last to leave was the corporal himself, and as he did so he fired a burst from his rifle into the club's ceiling. The club was in pandemonium. Sorcha left her ma and rushed to help some of the injured. An ambulance was called for two men, one with a cracked jaw and the other badly bruised along the thigh by a rubber bullet. Many others had minor injuries which a local doctor was called to deal with. Next day Sorcha and the other staff set about clearing up the havoc, ready for that evening's opening time.

Sorcha looked around the restaurant at the starched white linen, the gleaming cutlery and the waiters in their dark suits with white shirts and bow ties. It's a million miles from the old club, she thought, and smiled across at Frank.

'This is a nice treat,' she said.

Frank smiled back. He had successfully passed his exams and had driven Sorcha to the out-of-town restaurant in the second-hand but highly polished Volkswagen his dad had given him for passing.

After they had finished eating, Frank leant across and held Sorcha's hand. 'This is a special celebration,' he started.

'Because you've been so clever,' Sorcha cut in, squeezing his hand.

Frank looked into her eyes. 'I mean it could be a double celebration,' he said excitedly. 'Dad's got a friend in London who's got me a start in chambers over there, it's a real chance to learn the ropes where it matters.'

He hesitated a second or two, unable to fathom what Sorcha was thinking. 'I want... I thought we could get married, start a new life away from Belfast, away from all this,' he said, waving his other hand.

Sorcha was in turmoil. She liked Frank, had even thought of them getting married; but he had never talked before about leaving. She knew he had been upset that the civil rights campaigns had been superseded by the violence of a war situation, but to leave, was that the answer?

'Do you have to go to London?' she asked quietly.

Frank was adamant. 'I've already accepted the job, I've made up my mind. Don't you see the situation here is hopeless now – it's just guns against guns, we can't do anything.'

Sorcha slowly shook her head. 'I don't agree, Frank,' she said.

'You should have talked to me about it. But I'm not going to leave, this is my home.'

Frank became angry. 'You don't understand,' he said, as he usually did before launching into his explanations of the past few years' events.

Sorcha stood her ground, saying gently but firmly, 'Your understanding is different from mine, that's all.'

After an inconclusive argument, Frank went into a sulk and drove Sorcha home silently in the car. They saw each other a few times after this, but a barrier had grown between them and later in the year Frank left Belfast on his own to take up his new life in London.

Through her work in the club, Sorcha had increasingly come into contact with republican-minded people, and she began to feel that she should be doing something about the situation. In a way, her argument with Frank brought these feelings to a head. The civil rights days had seemed to pass her by, although she had supported the demands and taken part in some of the actions. The students and the professional people had thrust themselves into the forefront, distancing the movement from people like her. But now, with what was happening, she felt she had to do something. Since internment, since Seán's torture, since Bloody Sunday, it was to do with her.

If you did nothing it would still come to you, she thought; it would hit you between the eyes, hurt you, you couldn't escape it. Some tried to escape it though, pretended it wasn't there; they rode out the repression or got out altogether like Frank had done. She couldn't blame them, that was an instinct that most would follow, to ignore or escape. But others chose to fight, with whatever came to hand in most cases, even if the odds were great and the opposition appeared insurmountable.

Sorcha couldn't quite put her finger on it, why she increasingly felt the way she did. It was like a jigsaw: the history of her people, the oppressive state they had to live in, and what was happening now. When she put the pieces together it led her to one conclusion, this feeling that she should join the fight. She held back because fear would rise up too, but each time she thought about it, her feelings kept getting stronger.

As Sorcha was returning from the shop one evening with a bottle of milk, she bumped into the man from the end of the street. He asked how she was finding the job at the club. After a bit of chat, they were about to part when Sorcha blurted out that she wanted to help those who were fighting to change things.

The man smiled. 'I'll see if I can have a wee word with someone,' he promised.

A few days later, as Sorcha walked home from the club, a woman standing in a doorway called out to her. 'There's someone inside would like a word with you, love.'

Sorcha was motioned through to the small back kitchen and the door was pulled closed behind her. Sitting at the small kitchen table was Eileen, the woman who had helped her ma when Sorcha had been taken into the barracks for interrogation.

'Take a seat,' Eileen said, indicating the chair opposite. 'We hear you're interested in helping the war effort.'

Sorcha looked at her in surprise. 'Yes, I want to help,' she said.

'Why?' The question from Eileen came as a bit of a shock.

'Do I need a reason?' Sorcha asked.

Eileen leaned forward. 'If you want to join us, yes you do,' she said.

Sorcha took a deep breath and struggled to put her reasons into coherent form. She told about Bloody Sunday, seeing the people being shot off their own streets. How, on the bus back to Belfast that evening, there had been a subdued silence broken only by the odd whisper here or there. The expressions on the faces of those people who had participated in the march and witnessed the killings had told their own story. Frank, and those who had advocated peaceful protest as the only way forward, had worn looks of horror, helplessness and hopelessness. But as she had glanced around, Sorcha had seen the republicans with looks of grim determination. She had remembered the exchanges of banter and the songs as they had gone to Derry that morning and it was then that a sudden thought had come to her. What if the Provos were right? What if the Brits only listened when force was used?

The words started slowly, then came out in a rush. She told of the burning of Bombay Street, of internment and her brother being lifted and tortured; of her fears and her doubts as well as her feelings that something must be done to change the situation, fight the repression. Then her words started to dry up and she looked across at Eileen.

'My granny and granda, they fought in their time – and suffered for it too. The next generation, most of them anyway, just wanted to get on with their lives – even if they found that difficult, what with the discrimination and the peelers and the B-men and that. The civil rights struggle woke us all up, and gave us hope that we could get our rights by peaceful means. But now,' Sorcha shook her head, 'but now we either give in, or we fight. We're either off our knees – a risen people – or we're on them begging for mercy. There's no in-between any longer.' She looked up at Eileen again, 'I expect you think I'm all muddled up. I haven't put my reasons very clearly.'

Eileen smiled back. 'The reason I asked that question so bluntly is because we get people who want to join us for the wrong reasons,' she said. 'They've had a relative killed by loyalists and want revenge, or they've been beaten up by the Brits and want a gun to go out and shoot a soldier.'

Eileen leant forward as Sorcha listened. 'Such people we can understand, sympathise with them too, but those are not good enough reasons to join us. We are a disciplined organisation with a political motivation and ideology that goes back to Wolfe Tone and the United Irishmen.'

She looked at Sorcha. 'What you said, it's what we all think: we're not in a position yet to create what we would like to see. Now we just fight against what has been foisted on us: the Northern state, the Brits on the streets – I don't have to tell you. Anyway, your answer was the right one for us.' Eileen leaned back. 'What do you want to do?' she asked.

Sorcha shrugged: that was something she hadn't thought about.

Eileen smiled. 'I was at the meeting when your name came up. I said that I'd like to interview you – some of the men think we're only good for making tea. They see us as backup: we carry the guns, they fire the shots.'

She hesitated for a second, looking at Sorcha. 'There's a few of us women who think we should be up front, the same as the men, no differences.' Eileen smiled again. 'Sorry if that sounds like a lecture, what do you think?'

Sorcha smiled back even though her heart was thumping. 'I don't know what I could do, but I'm not putting myself forward to be kept in the background. I'd want to take the same risks as everyone else.'

Eileen looked delighted. 'Good on you,' she said, reaching across and clapping Sorcha on the shoulder. 'I'll put you forward. You should hear from us again soon.'

It was dark in the back of the van. The windows had been painted over in white, allowing in enough light to see, but stopping those inside from seeing out. Sorcha looked at the seven others; no one talked, as all were unsure who their companions were. Sorcha leant back, making herself comfortable, and drifted away into her thoughts.

Two weeks ago she had been informed that she had been accepted into the IRA, and that her first task was to go on a training course at a secret location. She had arranged a holiday and told her ma and friends that she was going to visit their relatives near Newry, then move on to Dublin.

Sorcha smiled, remembering the hospitality of her aunt and uncle. Finbar, her cousin, had met her off the Belfast bus and they chatted away as he drove her out to the smallholding.

Suddenly Finbar had muttered a curse, pointing to the road ahead. 'It's the UDR – a road block,' he said bitterly. 'I hope the bastards don't mess us about.'

As the pick-up slowed to a halt and a UDR man stepped forward, Sorcha was surprised to see a grin come over Finbar's face. The soldier had a clipboard in one hand while a sub-machine gun dangled from his other shoulder. Finbar wound down the window as the man approached.

'Hello, Jim,' Finbar called cheerfully to the soldier. 'How's about ye, the milk round doing all right this weather?'

The stoney look on the face of the UDR man did not change. 'Name and address?' he asked.

'Sure you know me name, you worked with me long enough,' answered Finbar, still smiling.

The soldier stared at Finbar, but the look on his face remained the same. 'Name and address,' he demanded again. 'Then you can open up the back till I take a wee look.'

The smile left Finbar's face as he gave the required information, adding his date of birth when asked.

As they drove past the end of the check-point, Sorcha looked quizzically at Finbar. 'Did you know that fellow?' she asked.

'I only worked with him for six years,' he replied sarcastically.

He looked at Sorcha and, seeing her interest, continued, 'It was a dairy, we collected the milk from the farms, bottled it, then delivered to the folks.'

Finbar glanced at Sorcha again. 'They got some new machinery in and decided to lay a few of us off. They'd treated our crowd okay up till then, we'd had no complaints, but it was us Catholics who got the push.'

Sorcha looked at him. 'What about the fellow who stopped us?' she asked.

Finbar concentrated on negotiating a bend in the road before answering. 'Ach, yer man, as I said I worked with him at the dairy. I knew him well, got on fine with him too. They kept him on.' He glanced at Sorcha again. 'He's doing well you know, he's still got the dairy job, he's in the UDR – part-time of course – and he works the farm with his da.'

Later on as Sorcha was chatting with her aunt in the house she mentioned the view they had over the valley.

Her aunt shook her head. 'View? Yes, lovely view, but the land this high up isn't up to much, you can only scratch a living off it.

'That land,' her aunt continued, pointing to the fertile-looking valley below, 'our people lived down there, till they were forced off it.' She looked at Sorcha. 'Ach, it was a long long time ago, but your uncle, he could still tell you how the planters got our good lands. We had to make do with this.'

After a couple of days Sorcha said her farewells and made her way to the arranged pick-up point at Dundalk.

'My name is Tully.' It was the first day at the training camp and the instructor was introducing himself. The van had deposited the volunteers at a small farm in a hilly area with woods and scrubland dotted around. Sorcha was billeted in a tiny back room with the other woman, Mairead from the Bogside in Derry. Now they were gathered in an outbuilding eyeing the instructor, who was a short middle-aged man with a slight paunch.

'I joined the IRA in the fifties,' Tully continued. 'I was about your age then, and my reasons for joining could have been described as a mixture of romanticism and bravado. I had read a bit of the history, I saw that the country needed to be united, and that the English presence had to be fought – so I had a go.'

Tully paused, looking the volunteers over. 'Then I was put in prison for a while, it was quite an education. Inside you meet all sorts, from street sweepers to professional people, and everything in between. You start to see that the country you live in is made up of all sorts of people with different customs and practices from yourself. You also begin to see the different social layers that exist in the country, and there is a great exchange of views. I was inside for a few years and you spend your time reading, discussing and thinking. You start to think for what, and just for whom, you are supposed to be fighting. In the past our movement was a coalition of different classes in our society: it was always the people of no property who predominated in the fighting, but it was left to the professional and business layers to control the political direction.'

Tully's voice became harsher. 'It was these people who shaped the Free State that produced the neo-colonial twenty-six counties, that works hand in glove with the Brits and the unionists in the north.'

Tully looked over the volunteers again and his voice softened. 'Traditionally our movement could be said to have as its foundation four "isms": nationalism, separatism, secularism and anti-sectarianism. Those four combined to make up the ideology of republicanism. The problem was that the politics and social aims of the movement were undefined. Modern republicanism was born on the streets of Dublin at Easter in 1916, when the Irish Republican Brotherhood joined forces with Connolly's Irish Citizen Army to rise up against Britain. As you know, the Easter rising was put down and Connolly was taken out with the rest and shot, but his writings joined those of Tone, Lalor, Mitchel and Pearse to form a basis for our politics. In other words, the socialism of Connolly joined the other "isms" to give republicanism an added dimension – a definite political direction towards a socialist republic.'

Tully's voice rose. 'We are a movement of working class people from the towns and country. We are not just fighting to get rid of something, we are also fighting to build something. We want a just society in a united thirty-two counties, where the ordinary folk, the people of no property, will have the say in how things go.'

Tully looked the volunteers over again. 'We are not like other armies, we do not promise you a good life. Instead we offer struggle, suffering and dislocation of family life. We offer imprisonment perhaps, or maybe death. It's not an easy life, there is no glamour, we are a secret army.'

His voice softened. 'If any one of you wants to leave at any time during this training, you can do so. We will shake hands, there will be no hard feelings on our side. We will keep quiet about you, all we will ask is that you do the same about us. We do not want anyone who is undecided, we need absolute commitment and dedication. When you leave here at the end of training, you'll leave as revolutionary soldiers in Oglaigh na hÉireann, the Irish Republican Army.'

The first two days passed quickly. There were lectures by Tully about republican ideology, the present situation and the background to it, and about the war and republican tactics and strategy against the British war machine.

On the third day Tully appeared carrying a long thin object wrapped in sacking and tied tightly with string. As the volunteers settled down, he slowly unwrapped it, then lifted the the object from the sacking. Sorcha felt a tightening in her stomach as Tully eyed the eight young volunteers, then held out the weapon in his hands.

'This is the Armalite 180 assault rifle. Its calibre is 5.56mm, its length is just over 36 inches and its weight with a full magazine is 7.75 pounds.'

He looked around the room and clicked the magazine into place. 'Some people in the North call it the widow-maker because of the amount of Brits that have been shot by this weapon. It can kill up to five hundred yards away and the bullets leave the muzzle at 3,250 feet per second.'

Tully rested the gun on the table. 'The AR-180 is a sister weapon to the M-16 that the Americans use in Vietnam. However there is an interesting tale to tell about that. American soldiers have been known to pick up and use an AK-47 captured from the NLF or North Vietnamese and throw away their Armalites. The reason is that this is quite a fragile weapon, so it can easily get jammed with dust or dirt.'

He patted the rifle. 'In Vietnam, in the jungle and the swamp, that is a big problem, but it's not to us here provided we look after the gun well. In fact the Armalite is a great little weapon for our type of conflict, urban guerilla warfare. We use it mainly for the one-shot snipe – it is ideally suited for that purpose.'

On the Friday morning Tully led the volunteers across some fields to a disused quarry overgrown with vegetation along its sides. At the bottom of one side was a small, almost flat, wooden hut, over which earth had been heaped and grass now grew, giving it the appearance from behind of a hillock.

'This is where we fire from,' Tully said. 'We have lookouts posted around in case anyone's about, and anyhow these walls muffle the sound.'

Little targets were placed on the far side of the quarry and Tully showed the volunteers how to load, where to lie in the hut, and how to aim and fire. Earlier in the week they had learned about explosives and Sorcha had felt uncomfortable, even though it hadn't been real material they had worked with. She had felt better working with the guns, stripping and assembling them again. The Armalite, especially, she had felt at ease with: it was so light and yet so precise, unlike some of the other weapons that had seemed quite ugly. She was glad to see Tully would be using the AR-180 for the firing, but her heart was still thumping when it came to her turn.

Tully knelt behind her as Sorcha loaded the rifle and then lay down, making herself comfortable in the firing position. As she brought the gun up to her shoulder she concentrated on remembering the instructions; then, looking through the sights, she swung the Armalite onto the target. She relaxed and breathed in, took up the slack in the trigger, then concentrating hard brought the sights into line with the bullseye and squeezed the trigger.

After her second shot, Sorcha glanced briefly behind her at Tully who was looking at the target through field-glasses. She had heard him instructing the others after one or two shots to move their aim.

Tully looked down at her. 'Carry on,' was all he said.

Sorcha fired off the rest of her shots, taking her time, her concentration blotting out everything else. As she got to her feet at the end, Tully glanced quizzically at her but did not say anything. Later back at the farmhouse he called Sorcha to one side to speak to her. He pulled a target from his pocket and started to smooth it out.

'You've shot before?' he asked.

Sorcha shook her head. 'No,' she answered.

Tully finished straightening out the target and looked at her.

'See that,' he said, indicating the target on which there were a number of small holes grouped around the centre black, with one hole through the centre itself. 'That's one of the best I've seen.'

'Beginner's luck,' said Sorcha with a smile. She counted the hits on the target. 'Look, there's only nine holes. I must have missed with one shot.'

Tully shook his head. 'I was watching with the glasses.' He pointed to the hole in the centre. 'See that one – it's a wee bit larger than the rest – your last two shots went through the same hole.'

On the final day of the course Tully gave his last lecture.

'I want you to imagine that you're Vietnamese, you've joined the liberation forces and you are lying in wait for American troops to appear. You've joined the NLF because you want to get back at the fat-cats who are exploiting and destroying your country. So an American soldier appears in the sights of your rifle. Who is it? Is it Tricky Dicky, the president? Is it a big fat businessman?'

Tully looked around the volunteers, shaking his head. 'No, it'll probably be a poor black from a slum area of some large city, whose ancestors were taken to America as slaves and who has been kicked around ever since.'

He looked them over again. 'But you'd better believe this – you still pull that trigger. Because if you don't, you might as well give up and go home. You have to know why you are fighting and who you are fighting. The Brits are no different, you won't get a banker or a politician for a target. It will be some poor unemployed working class kid, he may be black or even Irish. But you still have to pull that trigger because the uniform he wears represents the establishment. It's not him you are shooting but that system.'

'Irish Republican Army,' the man said, pushing the door and walking in as the woman who had answered the knock stepped back in surprise.

'We need your house for a wee while,' he continued. 'Keep quiet, don't panic, and you'll be all right.'

'Don't upset my man, he gets all excited when there's racing on the telly,' said the woman, chasing after the IRA man and pulling his sleeve.

Sorcha and the others followed as the woman led the man through to the front room where her husband sat staring at the TV screen.

'It's the Provies,' said the woman, but he did not look up.

The woman repeated her message, while her husband still stared at the screen.

'Jesus Christ! Can yous not wait till after the next race,' he said. 'I've bet on three in an accumulator and so far the first two have come up.'

The woman shook her head and the volunteers grinned at each other. 'You can sit there if you want,' said Kevin, the leader of the active service unit. 'But we'd better put a bit of rope around you – keep you in the clear if the Brits come.'

Kevin nodded to Liam and Padraig, who were to look after things on the ground floor, then moved to the stairs followed by Sorcha who carried a short oblong bundle under her arm. They made their way to the front bedroom and Kevin checked out the window while Sorcha undid the bundle. She took out the parts, laying them on the bed, then fitted them together to make up the Armalite. Kevin opened the window six inches at the bottom, then took the rifle from Sorcha and knelt down, gazing intently out of the gap. Suddenly the youth at the end of the street pulled a cigarette from a packet, lit it and moved off up the street.

'They're coming,' Kevin hissed, moving his position to get comfortable. Sorcha, standing motionless at the end of the bed, caught a vague outline of the first soldier through the curtains as Kevin slowly swung the Armalite up to a firing position.

'Yippee!' The shout from downstairs caused them both to jump.

'What the fuck?' exclaimed Kevin, motioning Sorcha to find out.

As she hurried to the top of the stairs, Liam appeared at the bottom and explained what had happened.

Sorcha hurried back to Kevin. 'It was your man downstairs, his third horse just won,' she said, barely able to suppress a smile.

Kevin tightened his grip on the rifle. He had been watching the soldiers and noticed one further back giving orders.

'I think there's an officer out,' he whispered to Sorcha, and moved his aim to take in the new target. This soldier was further away and Kevin had to move the Armalite six inches forward to give himself a better firing position. He aimed and took up the slack in the trigger. The front soldier, who was by now level with their window, noticed the slight movement of the Armalite's barrel tip and instantly brought his SLR up to his shoulder and fired two shots.

Kevin's finger was tightening on the trigger when the first of the heavy SLR bullets shattered the glass of the window in his face. The Armalite jerked slightly as he fired, diverting the bullet from the lower neck to the upper arm of his target, who spun around before collapsing onto the street. Sorcha, keeping low, pulled Kevin away from the window with one hand and grabbed the rifle in the other.

Kevin's face was bleeding: he hadn't been hit by a bullet but the shattered glass had cut him badly. 'My eyes, I can't see,' he gasped.

'We have to get out, the Brits will be here in seconds,' Sorcha said urgently. Fighting to overcome the feelings of panic, she took Kevin firmly by the arm and hurried him down the stairs. Liam and Padraig had tied the couple loosely to chairs and gagged them.

'You don't know who we were, we all wore masks,' Liam shouted to the couple, as he and Padraig joined Sorcha and Kevin rushing to the back door. With the officer wounded, it was taking the patrol some time to calm down, but the radio operator had garbled out a message that would bring any soldiers in the area racing towards the location of the shooting. Liam jumped into the driving seat of the getaway car while Sorcha and Padraig helped Kevin into the back. Suddenly, a 'pig' armoured personnel carrier turned the corner and swung into the entrance of the back alley.

Kevin and Padraig were already in the car, with Sorcha holding the Armalite in one hand about to follow. Instead she slammed the door.

'I'll hold them back, yous get away,' she shouted.

Liam hesitated but Sorcha leant towards him. 'Get going, don't argue,' she yelled, and this time the driver pulled away fast on screeching tyres.

Sorcha turned back towards the pig, raised the rifle and fired two quick shots. The first bullet bounced off the bonnet of the personnel carrier and smashed into the steel body of the vehicle above the driving window; the second hit the armoured glass directly in front of the driver, starring it on impact. The driver, ducked instinctively and braked, jerking the steering wheel over in the process. The armoured personnel carrier careered into a wall and ground to a halt.

Sorcha looked behind her and saw her comrades' car disappear safely around the corner. Turning back, she could see soldiers carrying SLRs jumping out of the rear of the pig, so she quickly found cover through the gate of the house they had just left. She was glancing around desperately, thinking, with an increasing sense of panic, that she was trapped, when she noticed a woman beckoning her from the open gate of the backyard across the way. It's my one chance, Sorcha thought, and tensing herself she suddenly bounded across, loosing a burst of gunfire in the soldiers' direction as she did so. One soldier braver than the rest jumped up and fired back in return, and the bullets ricocheted up the road behind her just as Sorcha gained the safety of the backyard.

The woman hustled Sorcha straight through the house, slamming the gate and doors shut behind them, and then pointed to another house across the next street. 'Over there,' she said. 'The door will be open – just push it, you'll be helped inside.'

Her heart still pounding, Sorcha ran across the next street, pushed the house door open and disappeared inside.

Another woman appeared immediately. 'Right, break down the gun and put it in this,' she said, holding up a long narrow bag made from the cut-off leg of a pair of jeans. 'Then get that gear off, I'll get you a change of clothes.'

As the woman hurried off, Sorcha quickly stripped the Armalite and placed the parts in the bag, then removed her combat jacket and trousers. Her beret fell off as she removed her jersey, so she removed the pins from her hair and, shaking her head, allowed the dark tresses to cascade down.

'Jesus, Mary and Saint Joseph!' The woman had returned and now stood open-mouthed staring at Sorcha. 'I thought you were a wee lad,' she added, holding out the men's clothing she had brought. The woman recovered her composure. 'My eldest daughter is fifteen but she's quite big. Come upstairs and we'll see if there's anything that will fit.'

Sorcha followed the woman to the daughter's room and managed to squeeze into a short tight skirt, a blouse and a pair of high heeled shoes. The woman then put Sorcha's clothes into a bag and laid the other bag with the armalite parts in it on top. 'I've a good place for these where the Brits will never find them,' she said.

She then thrust a shopping basket into Sorcha's hands. 'Right, we have to get you out the area,' she said. 'Just say you're going shopping. Walk out the front, turn right along the street till the end and you're into the Falls.'

Stifling Sorcha's attempts to thank her, the woman grasped her arm. 'Good luck, take care, love, the Brits will be out in force now,' she whispered, as Sorcha opened the door and disappeared down the street.

'What did the groupie see when she looked up Mick Jagger's trouser leg?' Corporal Bruce was trying to chat up the women searchers, who giggled and shook their heads.

'Two stones and a pretty thing,' he answered, laughing. The two women looked away and pretended not to laugh.

Corporal Bruce, Billy, Monroe and two other soldiers were

on gate duty on the west side of the city centre. A ring of steel had been erected around this commercial area with gates at various intervals providing the only way in or out. Everyone was searched coming in: soldiers searching the men, with civilian female searchers for the women. The soldiers regarded the duty as tedious so they livened it up in any way they could.

'My God, look at the top kit on that,' shouted Corporal Bruce as a young woman approached.

'She'd never fall flat on her face,' muttered another squaddie.

Corporal Bruce turned to the women searchers. 'Hey, how's about a swop, we'll search the women and yous can search the men,' he said.

The women ignored him.

'Come on, you'd like that really,' he persisted, then turned back to the soldiers. 'We'd all like that, wouldn't we? Except for Marilyn here,' Corporal Bruce indicated Monroe. 'He likes searching the men.'

Monroe blushed and looked away.

'Ach, leave him alone, you're always picking on him,' said one of the woman searchers who had a slight squint in one eye.

Corporal Bruce turned back to the women. 'Okay, what's long and thin, it's covered in skin, it's red in parts, and you shove it into tarts?'

The women looked away in disgust.

'There you are, they've got real dirty minds,' said Corporal Bruce. 'The answer is – a stick of rhubarb,' he shouted triumphantly, laughing at the women.

The woman with the squint looked at her friend. 'It would take a prick like him to know a joke like that,' she whispered.

The soldiers heard her whisper and Corporal Bruce, glaring at the women, lifted his right leg slightly, strained his body and emitted a loud sloppy fart.

'You dirty bastard,' called Billy. 'A rat must have crawled up your arse and died.'

Corporal Bruce took no notice, still staring at the women who had looked away. 'Hey,' he called out to them. 'Do farts have lumps in them?'

The women still looked away.

'Cause if they don't, I think I've shit myself,' the corporal continued.

The woman searcher with the squint looked at him angrily. 'You're disgusting,' she said.

Corporal Bruce grinned. 'Just when I'd fallen in love with you too,' he said. 'I just told the lads here how lovely you are.'

The corporal turned to the soldiers for a second and winked, before turning back to the woman again. He went down on one knee. 'Your eyes are like pools,' he said to the woman. 'Football pools – one home, one away.' Corporal Bruce laughed loudly as the woman turned away blushing a deep red.

'You've upset her,' accused the other woman.

Just then a landrover roared up to the check-point carrying Sergeant Wallace and a driver.

'There's been a shooting up the Falls,' the sergeant shouted, and told Corporal Bruce and Billy to jump in the back. When they did so, the vehicle roared off, proceeding up the Falls Road and stopping at a street end.

'Right,' said Sergeant Wallace, jumping out. 'We're trying to set up a cordon around the location of the incident. We'll cover this end of the street and check anyone trying to come out.'

The soldiers took up positions. Corporal Bruce lay down on the pavement against a side wall, facing up the street. The driver did the same on the other side, while Sergeant Wallace and Billy prepared to stop and search.

Sorcha moved awkwardly along the street, conscious that the clothes and the shoes felt too small, when suddenly these thoughts were driven from her mind. A Brit landrover had screeched to a halt at the end of the street, and soldiers had jumped out and taken up positions on either side of the street. Sorcha's heart was beating hard. She hesitated for a fraction of a second, then went on walking towards the soldiers.

'Cor, this is a bit of all right,' hissed Corporal Bruce to Billy as Sorcha approached.

Billy motioned her to stop as Corporal Bruce settled himself on the pavement, leering up at her.

'Where are you off to?' Billy asked her.

'Just some shopping,' Sorcha replied, holding out the basket so he could look inside.

Billy was just about to ask for her name and address when Corporal Bruce cut in. 'Hey doll, if that skirt was any shorter, I'd be able to see what you had for breakfast.'

'Corporal Bruce!' The unit lieutenant had suddenly appeared behind them. 'One of our chaps gets shot by mick terrorists and all you can do is chat up the local crumpet.'

The radio, carried by the soldier following the officer, crackled out a message. The lieutenant turned inquiringly.

'They want the cordons moved in a bit to the next junction, then they'll conduct house-to-house searches, sir,' the radio operator said.

'Right men, get ready to move positions,' snapped the officer. He turned back to the operator. 'Try and get a description of the suspect – someone was seen, I believe.'

The radio crackled again for a period, then the operator reported to the lieutenant. 'He was wearing olive combat gear and a black beret. They said he wasn't very tall but he was brawny, sir.'

A grin came on the operator's face. 'They said he was built like a brick shithouse, sir, and he was firing bullets faster than John Wayne.'

Sorcha stood silently as the soldiers piled into the landrover and moved off up the street. Later that evening she made contact with her IRA unit's intelligence officer. Sorcha learned that the Brit searches had found nothing. Liam, Padraig and Kevin had escaped safely, but Kevin's eyes needed a doctor's attention and he had been moved over the border where he would receive treatment.

Sorcha still felt herself shaking when she thought of the situation she had just survived, but there was something else that bothered her too. It was the soldier who had stopped her: somewhere at the back of her mind she knew she had seen him before. Then she remembered the Brits who had lifted Seán: he had been one of them then, she was sure. And that night in the club when soldiers had come in and wrecked the place, she thought she had seen him then. But there was more than that. She had met him somewhere before all this had happened, before the North had erupted, before the Brits had come onto the streets. It was funny, she thought, with most people whom you think you should know, you can close your eyes and form a mental picture of them. You can recall their face and features and that can help you to place them, to remember where you had met them. With the soldier it was different. Try as she might, all she could conjure up was the uniform and the cap badge with its crown on top. His face and features remained just a blur.

As he trudged along, Spoons McCann was thinking of the note Teresa had stuffed into the top pocket of his jacket.

'I don't want you moping around under my feet,' she had said, but he knew that was only her way of giving him permission to go out for a drink. Spoons fingered the note, then pulled it out and peered at it: one pound, he muttered to himself. He knew that Teresa gave him as much as she could, but how far would a quid go? He'd always liked a drink but now since the accident it was his only way to escape, to forget what had happened.

He smiled as he remembered that night in the pub when he'd pulled the spoons out of his pocket and rattled out a few tunes. Suddenly a pint had been sitting in front of him, followed by another and then a few more. He chuckled to himself; no bother at all, at least he could still do that. He'd done okay, he played a few tunes and earned a drink or two. But times were hard, people didn't have the money and he'd found the free drinks running out as sympathy lapsed. He'd move on then, find another pub and start over again. He'd moved further and further afield, and now there were no more pubs left down the Falls that he had not visited.

Spoons trudged down to the bottom of the road, moved through a deserted Smithfield Market and walked on till he found a new pub that looked promising. He peeped round the door, then sidled up to the bar and bought a pint with the pound note. He carried his drink and shuffled to a round of seats at the far end of the room, occupied by three men at one end. Spoons sat down at the end away from the men and quietly sipped his pint. When he only had a little beer left he slowly pulled the spoons from his pocket and rattled out 'Seven Drunken Nights'. Spoons smiled at the men and they stopped talking and grinned back.

When he finished the tune one of the men raised his glass. 'Give us the "Sash",' he shouted across.

Spoons looked at him uncomprehendingly and shook his head.

The three men looked at him. 'Fuck all good you are,' said the man. 'Give us the "Green Grassy Slopes" then.'

Spoons racked his brains for the tune but could not recall it and shook his head again. The man who had made the request said something to his companions who laughed. He was about to continue when the thin-faced man beside him placed a hand on the man's arm, then moved across to sit next to Spoons. The thin-faced man looked at Spoons and smiled.

'If you don't know my friend's songs, you must know "Seán South", so give us that,' he said.

Spoons looked at the man; something at the back of his mind told him that things weren't right, but he couldn't think why. The thin-faced man beside him still had a fixed smile on his face as Spoons started up.

Sorcha stood silently sipping her drink; her ma sat with an arm around Teresa's shoulder comforting her. On a table in the middle of the room lay the coffin as a steady stream of friends and relatives visited to pay their last respects. Sorcha remembered this same room when Gerry had been killed by the Brits. Then the coffin had been open and the boy's face, although pale, had looked strangely at peace. Now the coffin remained firmly closed: the doctor had explained to Teresa that the gunshot wound to her husband's head would be distressing to view. He hadn't mentioned the multiple stab wounds, the cross and the letters IRA scratched on his back, or the genitals roasted with a blowlamp. Later Sorcha helped Teresa's remaining children prepare for bed; gently she brushed Siobhán's hair and talked to her about what she was learning at school. Next day, amid constant showers of rain that swept down between the hills towards the sea, Spoons McCann was laid to rest beside his son Gerry.

'The sarge, he's been shot.'

Billy was lying on his bunk thinking of home when the door burst open and an excited soldier rushed in.

'What! The dirty Irish bastards,' gasped Billy, heaving himself upright.

The soldier stopped and glanced at Billy. 'Listen, but it wasn't the micks this time,' he said.

Billy and the others looked at each other bewildered as the soldier paused for a second, then continued, 'It was Golly that shot him.'

'But why?' Billy and a few other squaddies asked the question at the same time.

The soldier looked around at his audience. 'The sarge was dropping off a patrol from a lorry and he told Golly to be the tail-end-charlie again. Well, Golly said he was always put on that — that it was the most dangerous position and he wouldn't do it anymore.'

Billy and his friends stared back with startled faces as the soldier went on. 'Then the sarge shouted at him, told him to stand to attention and say the verses he'd been taught. Golly just seemed to flip his lid. He brought up his SLR and shot the sarge in the guts.'

'Fucken nig-nogs.' Corporal Bruce had entered the room behind the soldier. 'This is what happens when we let them into the army.'

'He was descended from the Covenanters you know,' Monroe spoke quietly from the corner of the room.

The rest of the squaddies looked at him.

'Who was? The sarge you mean?' Billy asked.

Monroe shook his head. 'No, Robertson I meant,' he said, then seeing the disbelieving looks added, 'he told me so.'

Corporal Bruce glared at him. 'What would you know, you fucken nancy boy, you're talking through your arse again as usual.'

Corporal Bruce was about to continue when a voice along the corridor was heard calling on him to report to the lieutenant. When he left, Billy turned back to Monroe. 'What were you on about?' he asked curiously.

'We were on sentry duty once,' said Monroe. 'Me and Robertson, he told me a bit about himself.'

All the soldiers stared at Monroe as he went on. 'His family came over in the fifties, said his dad had fought against the Germans like.'

Monroe hesitated, but they were all still listening and no one else spoke. 'Their history had been passed down from generation to generation. He said the word was that they were descended from a black woman who was taken to the West Indies as a slave, and a white man who had suffered the same fate.'

'You must be joking,' another soldier shouted across. 'There weren't any white slaves.'

Monroe looked at him. 'I'm just telling you what Robertson told me,' he explained. 'He said that some whites had been sent out as slaves after getting into trouble in this country. He said their white man had had his left ear cut off as a punishment before he was shipped out. The man was called Robertson and he'd been captured after some fight the Covenanters had lost. After a while out there he was given his freedom and farmed a bit of land. He took up with this black woman and after he'd been free a while he bought her freedom too. They set up together and that's who Robertson's ancestors were. He said when his parents went to Glasgow they sort of looked upon it as coming home.'

'Were you two fucking bum chums?' Corporal Bruce had returned and stood in the doorway shouting at Monroe. 'Let me tell you, that nigger friend of yours is going to be sorry he was ever born, no matter who his fucken ancestors were.'

Monroe went silent and looked down at the floor. Corporal Bruce turned to Billy to tell him that the lieutenant wanted to see him now.

Sorcha held herself rigid as the constant file of people passed through murmuring words of comfort to Eileen's parents. A tri-colour flag covered the bottom half of the coffin on which were laid a black beret and gloves. Sorcha choked back her tears as she stood in her uniform of combat jacket and trousers with a beret, dark glasses, and a black handkerchief hiding her face bandit-style. She and her active service unit had volunteered to provide this guard of honour for her friend and comrade-in-arms, and tomorrow they would provide the firing party at the funeral.

Memories of Eileen kept flashing through Sorcha's mind. She remembered a few months ago when a bombing had gone tragically wrong with civilians killed and injured; warnings had been given but were not acted on by the authorities.

Eileen had refused to use that as an excuse. 'We must accept our part of the blame and do our very best to ensure it does not happen again,' she had said.

The tears had rolled down her cheeks and Sorcha had held her close, whispering words of comfort. Eileen's death had resulted from her determination to honour the pledge she had made not to risk civilian lives on operations. Eileen and a male comrade had been about to plant a bomb at a target but had become worried by the amount of people in the vicinity. They had decided to move the bomb back to base but on their return journey it had exploded, killing them both.

Sorcha remembered that some of the male volunteers had not been keen on her taking charge of the sniping unit after Kevin had gone south for treatment for his eyes. But the men within her unit had supported her, saying they had seen what she could do. They had not expected to see Sorcha again after leaving her facing a load of Brits.

'If that had been a fellow they'd have been singing songs about him up and down the Falls by now,' Eileen had said.

She had argued persistently that Sorcha should now take charge. 'Mao in China has a saying, "women hold up half the sky",' she had said. That meant, Eileen explained, that women were half the population, half the human resources. If you ignored them or relegated them to a background role, then that was a waste of those resources and only a fool would do that.

Billy stretched out on his bunk and rubbed his eyes. He had been dozing but a door slamming had woken him. He settled back and closed his eyes again but could not get back to sleep. He'd just had this vivid dream which kept running through his mind. That woman had been in it, the one he'd stopped in the street after the shooting incident. He knew he'd seen her before, but for the life of him he couldn't remember where. Still, they all got to look alike after a while, the paddies. They all hate us, and the women are the worst. She'd been polite enough then, in the street, but given half a chance she would have been hurling abuse and throwing stones just as quickly as the rest of them.

The dream had been strange and a little disturbing. He had been walking down a street, just like the ones around here, when two army landrovers had passed by. He raised his hand in greeting but the soldiers gave him hostile glances and one swung his rifle towards Billy, peering at him over the sights. Surprised by this reaction, he looked down to discover he was wearing jeans and a tee-shirt, not his uniform. Puzzled, he glanced at the wall behind and saw he was in Glasgow and not Belfast as he had thought. Written in large white letters on the wall were the words 'Free Scotland!' He walked on and turning a corner saw, a little way ahead, an army checkpoint. The soldiers had stopped a woman and were questioning her. It was her: the woman Billy had stopped in the street, the one he recognised from somewhere. As he got closer he could hear the soldiers, with English accents, yelling abuse at the woman. Billy had felt puzzled, ashamed, and finally angry. He'd stopped and moved back into the shadow of the wall and that was when the noise had wakened him.

Billy yawned and looked at his uniform hanging on the locker door: the second stripe had just been sewn on the arm of his jacket. He smiled ruefully: they say every cloud has a silver lining, he thought. The sarge gets the chop, then Corporal Bruce gets made up to acting sergeant and himself to acting corporal. Billy remembered a few days ago when they'd just heard of Sergeant Wallace's shooting and he'd been called to see the lieutenant. He'd gone to the unit office and found the door ajar with voices coming from inside; it was the lieutenant and the captain who was second in command of the company. Billy had hesitated a moment, listening to their conversation.

'Did you enjoy your weekend? I hear you visited the Farquarsons,' asked the captain.

'Oh, all right,' the lieutenant replied.

'I hear they've got a pretty daughter,' continued the captain.

'Rhondy,' said the lieutenant. 'Yes, she's not bad.'

'Well, how did you get on, you randy sod? Did you get to bury the baldy fellow?' queried the captain.

'Give us a chance, that was my first visit,' pleaded the lieutenant. 'But they've asked me back, so I'll be working on it,' he chuckled.

Billy had knocked on the door and was told to enter. He did so and saluted, then he was told about his promotion.

'Temporary, till we see how you get on,' said the captain. 'If you can't handle it, perhaps we'll have to draft someone else in. If you can, perhaps it'll become permanent.'

Billy stretched himself: it's okay for them, he thought, visiting unionist families who regard the army as saviours. All the squaddies got was a disco now and again, if they were lucky, in some tacky hall in a loyalist area.

'Hey! How do we know that those IRA fuckers are all little runts?' The question was shouted out by the soldier on the bunk above Monroe.

There was silence for a few seconds, then the soldier gave the answer gleefully. 'Because of that song they all sing, "Soldiers are Wee".' He jumped down from the bunk dressed only in his Y-fronts, and putting a hand over his privates, thrust them towards Monroe who was lying on his bunk. 'Hey Marilyn, do you use knacker lacquer?' he asked. Turning to the rest of the room still clutching his privates with one hand, he put the other hand on his waist and adopted a lisping voice. 'Use knacker lacquer – it adds lustre to your cluster,' he said, to laughs from the rest of the squaddies.

Billy looked at his watch and jumped up. It was time to start getting the men ready, there was an IRA funeral to patrol.

'That's bound to be trouble,' Acting Sergeant Bruce had said.

At the briefing the CO had said they were to ensure that no shots were fired over the coffins. 'The Protestants won't like it,' he had said. 'And I want the hides of anyone who tries.'

The CO had accepted an invitation to visit a well-to-do unionist family at the weekend and didn't want them making any sarcastic remarks about his men's ability to deal with the 'taigs', which was how his hosts usually referred to the people of the Falls Road.

The rain had stopped and sunshine was breaking through the clouds as the cortege made its way slowly up the Falls Road. An IRA honour guard marched alongside the two coffins, followed by a crowd of several thousand mourners. The Brits were out in force also; soldiers and peelers lined the route while others, clustered around vehicles, waited up side streets as backup in case of trouble. A military helicopter hovered low overhead, keeping pace with the procession. Sorcha, Liam and Padraig walked along with the crowd holding wreaths. A large Brit presence had been expected and a plan had been worked out to counteract it. As the line of people swung into Milltown Cemetery the honour guard held back, letting the coffins proceed followed by the crowd. The Brits were confused; they had been closely watching the guard, expecting them at any minute to try to fire a volley of shots over the coffins of their comrades. About halfway to the freshly dug graves, the coffins halted and were quickly surrounded by the crowd who formed a dense mass around them.

Sorcha, Liam and Padraig passed their wreaths to others and quickly made their way into a certain area of the massed crowd. They knelt down as combat jackets, berets, dark glasses and black handkerchiefs were thrust towards them. When they stood again, adjusting their new outfits, Webley revolvers were pushed into their hands. The three stepped out of the crowd into the circle that had been left around the coffins and assembled into a line. Sorcha shouted out her orders, the guns were raised to the sky and three volleys of shots rang out to cheers from the crowd around them.

'Get those fenian bastards – get into them!' Acting Sergeant Bruce seemed beside himself with rage as he screamed out his orders. The soldiers had been taken by surprise but were determined to rectify this by capturing those responsible. Now the crowd was so densely packed that Billy and his squad had to force a way through.

'Use your batons!' Billy yelled, as the people refused to shift in front of them. Under this new onslaught the mourners started to fall back, allowing the soldiers to move forward slowly but steadily.

Aware that the Brits would try to rush in and capture them, Sorcha and her comrades dashed back into the crowd as soon as the shots had been fired. The helicopter was buzzing around overhead like a demented hornet, and Sorcha could see the disturbances at the back of the crowd as the Brits tried to force a way through. Once in the crowd again, Sorcha, Liam and Padraig knelt down, and a scrum developed round them as the jackets, berets, glasses, handkerchiefs and revolvers were snatched from them to vanish into the seething mass of people. As Sorcha stood up, the wreath was thrust back into her hands and the procession started off again, easing the pressure of the crowd who gradually reassembled into ranks following the coffins.

Billy's squad was the first into the centre of the crowd. People now moved out of the way if they were threatened, but otherwise acted as if the soldiers did not exist. Another squad arrived, with Acting Sergeant Bruce in their midst bawling orders to scrutinise the crowd and try to find the gunmen. Billy and the rest of the soldiers made their way backwards and forwards peering into the ranks of mourners.

Sorcha, Liam and Padraig joined the front rank of the procession along with the others holding wreaths, and the honour guard resumed their position alongside the coffins. The funeral continued as if nothing had happened, despite the presence of the Brits

pushing their way arrogantly through the crowds glaring to and
fro as they did so.

Sorcha leaned back in the armchair; she felt drained, the funeral
had been a traumatic experience. Tears filled her eyes as she
thought of Eileen; it just didn't seem possible she would never see
her friend again.

'Come on,' said her ma, standing in the doorway. 'You
promised to give Siobhán some more lessons.'

Sorcha got reluctantly to her feet. Ach well, she thought, perhaps it wouldn't do any harm, it might take her mind off things
and she had promised the lessons.

Before Victor had left he had given Sorcha a small portable
typewriter. 'It'll keep your hand in till you get back to this type of
work,' he had said. She had kept it in a cupboard in her bedroom
but rarely used it.

One day she had been tapping out a letter when Siobhán had
come in and stood silently watching.

'Could you teach me?' she had asked shyly when Sorcha had
finished.

Teresa welcomed them in and cleared the table by the front
window for Sorcha to put the typewriter on. The two mothers sat
by the fire talking while Sorcha sat beside Siobhán at the table,
watching the girl going over what she had been taught before.
She's so like me, how I used to be, Sorcha thought, smiling to
herself as she remembered her own schooldays. She leaned forward and patted Siobhán's arm encouragingly as the girl tapped
away.

Acting Sergeant Bruce pulled the tab from the can of McEwan's
Export and took a long drink. He looked at the empty cans litter-
ing the floor and kicked out at them with his foot, sending several

skidding to the opposite end of the room. The CO was not amused, he had been told. The IRA firing party at the funeral had been shown on the local TV to howls of outrage from the unionists.

'Fuck yous – you bastards,' he said angrily to himself as he drained the last dregs, then crushed the can in his hand and flung it violently away before making his way to find his men.

'I want yourself and three men, one of them a driver,' he shouted to Billy, who looked back questioningly.

'The CO's doing his bollocks about today – we're going on a little recce to see what we can see,' Bruce explained, before turning and going out the door muttering, 'I'll make some of them cunts pay for this, if it's the last thing I do.'

Sorcha was glad she had come out. Siobhán, an attentive pupil, was quickly picking up the basics of typing. Teresa had gone through to the kitchen to make a cup of tea when she poked her head back around the door.

'Could you run down to the shop and get a bottle of milk?' she shouted across to Siobhán.

'Ach mammy, just when I'm getting on great, look what I've just written,' the girl said, pulling the piece of paper from the typewriter and holding it up.

Sorcha smiled. 'I'll go and get the milk,' she said.

'Not at all, you stay where you are, love,' Teresa said, then turned to Siobhán. 'The money's in my purse – we'll have a look at what you've written when you get back.'

Billy sat in the front of the landrover beside the driver as they cruised the streets of little houses. Acting Sergeant Bruce had appeared gripping a rubber bullet gun and insisted on sitting in the back of the vehicle. The rain had started again, a gentle drizzle at first, then heavy showers sweeping down. The driver switched on the wipers as he turned off the Springfield Road into Clonard. The soldiers peered out into the dark streets, with Sergeant Bruce cursing the rain which would keep most people indoors. Suddenly two young men appeared at a corner. Sergeant Bruce swiftly raised the rubber bullet gun, but already the distance was too great and anyway the alarmed youths scuttled off up an alley.

'Fucken Irish bastards,' Sergeant Bruce muttered in frustration, when one of the other soldiers, who had been peering out the front, hissed that someone was coming up on the left. Bruce braced himself, raising the rubber bullet gun as he did so. He nearly missed the small figure hurrying along close to the front of the houses. His eyes caught the movement of the small white object the person held, helping him to zero in. Acting Sergeant Bruce leaned forward, tilting the gun into position, and fired.

Sorcha was sitting looking wistfully out the window; she had just noticed the rain when the landrover came into view.

Poor sods, she was thinking, even if they were Brits, out on a night like this, when the sound of the rubber bullet gun came in a dull report. Before she could gather her thoughts, the landrover had passed out of sight, but she strained her eyes to see what the target could have been.

'What's happening?' Teresa shouted across anxiously, just as Sorcha saw a spreading pool of white slide off the pavement opposite into the gutter. Because of the darkened streets Sorcha could not see anything else, but the realisation hit her like a thunderbolt.

'Siobhán!' she cried. Jumping up, she dashed out the door and was across the street in a flash – followed by her ma and the now alarmed Teresa. As she approached the spot where the milk from the smashed bottle had run, Sorcha could see the outline of a small figure collapsed against the wall. Tiny rivulets of red flowed through the milk and soaked away with it into the gutter.

Siobhán was kept alive for another three days on a life support machine in the Royal Victoria Hospital. The rubber bullet that killed her had been fired from five yards range. It had left the gun at one hundred and sixty miles per hour and hit her squarely on the head. After bitter protests by local people, a Brit press officer released a statement saying that baton rounds had been fired after an army patrol came under attack in a riot situation. That was how the incident was reported in the British papers.

Five days after the shooting Siobhán joined her da and her brother in the family plot in Milltown Cemetery. About a week later Teresa brought around the typewriter, which Sorcha had forgotten about. She also silently handed over a piece of typing paper. Sorcha saw it was the piece Siobhán had been working on before she had gone out. As she read it tears trickled down her cheeks:

I am Siobhán McCann
I am twelve years old
I live in Belfast.

Billy could feel the sweat oozing from his armpits, but he did not slacken his pace. He knew it wasn't just the walking that was causing the sweat; even on days in the middle of winter squaddies would return with their shirts sticking to their backs. The file of soldiers passed a house with the front window open and Billy could hear the Coronation Street signature tune drifting out. Sitting down in front of the telly for the night, he thought enviously. It was at times like this that he asked himself what he was doing here.

He glanced back, then scanned the road ahead. I must concentrate, he told himself, and cast all other thoughts from my mind. 'Lose concentration – and you could lose your life.' That's what the instructors at Tin City had said, and out on these streets you took that sort of advice to heart. The radio crackled behind him, and as Billy turned the operator gave a thumbs up sign.

'The 'Gers have scored – Colin Stein,' the radio man shouted across.

The news cheered Billy up: it was a Rangers versus Celtic match again and he had arranged for progress reports to be transmitted to his patrol. Billy hesitated for a second as a group of locals walked past. He looked at their resentful faces, they had this way of looking at you that sent shivers down your spine. They ignored you then took a quick glance, but it was like they were taking a note of you for later. Billy shook his head. Concentrate, get these thoughts out of your mind, he kept telling himself; concentrate, concentrate.

Billy took up a covering position as the soldier in front raced across a junction into another street. As Billy tensed himself to make the sprint over himself, he heard a commotion behind and quickly looked around. Some local kids they had passed minutes before playing football in the street had now gathered behind Monroe who was the tail-end-charlie. The children were chanting and shouting at the soldier, who was walking backwards keeping his eyes on the street to the rear of the patrol. Billy swore under his breath, then shouted at Monroe and the soldier in front of him to hurry forward to the junction. As the soldiers approached, Billy waved them past, watching till they reached the other side of the crossing. Then Billy turned suddenly towards the children who had now gathered behind him. 'Fuck off, or you'll get a boot up your arses,' he snarled, jabbing his rifle towards the children who fell back in alarm.

Billy then turned and ran quickly to the street where his patrol now waited. The children regrouped and stood at the end of their street, chanting a rhyme which Billy's ears just caught before he moved out of sight:

> We're on our way to Wembley,
> The Brits are in the entry,
> They can't get out,
> The 'RA's about.

A woman answered Sorcha's knock on the door and looked in surprise at the group standing on her doorstep.

'Irish Republican Army,' said Sorcha. 'We need your house for a wee while.'

The woman stepped back to let them enter, and Liam and Padraig moved in swiftly to check the rooms. Sorcha stayed beside the stairs holding a wrapped oblong object, and minutes later Liam returned.

'There's just the two of them, we'll take them in the kitchen and get ready to tie them up,' he said, then smiled. 'We'll have a cup of tea while we're waiting. One of their daughters went to school with Padraig, so they're chatting away just the thing.'

'Make sure you'll be ready,' said Sorcha, turning and making her way up the stairs.

'We'll be ready, don't you worry,' said Liam, then asked if she needed any help.

Sorcha shook her head and proceeded to the top of the house where she checked the rooms, then made her way to the front bedroom. She carefully unwound the wrappings from her bundle and laid the Armalite parts on the bed. She slowly snapped the sections together till the rifle was assembled; she checked the magazine, then thrust that home also. She left the weapon on the bed and moved to the window opening it six inches from the sill. She took up the gun again and peered along it out through the gap, till she was sure she would have no trouble finding her target. She checked the safety catch and jerked back the cocking handle, letting it go zipping forward, forcing a bullet into the chamber. Sorcha checked the rifle over again, then laid it gently on the bed before moving back to the window. She pushed the net curtains a bit to one side, and stood staring out through the gap up the street.

As Billy moved into the next street, he quickly cast a glance around. All the men were in position, so he moved past Monroe, the other soldier and the radio operator, then indicated to the patrol to move forward again. Two women were chatting on a doorstep but moved inside as the soldiers approached, slamming the door. Billy heard the radio crackle again and turned around; the operator scowled and shook his head giving a thumbs down sign.

'The fucken fenians have equalised,' he said crossly. 'That bastard Macari got it – you'd have thought big Greig would have crunched him up by now.'

Billy shrugged his shoulders. 'I had a feeling this wasn't going to be my day,' he said, turning to move off. He glanced at his watch and turned back again. 'Tell them we're in Indian country, moving along the Kashmir Road. When we reach Bombay, we'll set up a P-check for a bit, then move back to base.'

As the women who had been chatting moved inside and shut the door, Sorcha, gazing down from the window, felt a tightening in her stomach. She stood for a few seconds fighting to control her emotions, then hurried to the top of the stairs and shouted to Liam waiting below that the Brits were coming. She moved back to the room, picked up the Armalite from the bed, then knelt down slowly by the window and looked intently up the street.

The first soldier appeared, his head nodding from side to side as he scanned the street and rooftops ahead. Another soldier appeared after him, then another two close together, the rear one carrying a radio pack.

Sorcha inched the Armalite up into position. As she peered along the sights she saw the radio man say something to the one in front. This soldier said something in reply to the operator, who then started to speak into his radio. That's the one giving orders, Sorcha thought; he's just told the radio man to relay some message.

She remembered Tully's instructions. 'Don't look at the face – it's not the man you're firing at. You're shooting the uniform and all it stands for.'

Sorcha concentrated on the Armalite, clicking off the safety catch and steadying the sights on the target. She breathed in, let part of the breath out and took up the slack in the trigger. Holding her breath and with total concentration, she zeroed in exactly to the centre of her target and squeezed the trigger.

Billy looked up at the starry sky. Ach well, it wasn't such a bad evening, he thought; perhaps Rangers would get stuck in and get a win. His grip tightened on his SLR. I'm doing it again, letting my mind wander, Billy was thinking, when the Armalite bullet hit him a sledgehammer blow at the base of his neck. He did not remember falling. One minute he was striding along, the next he was choking on his own blood, lying face down on a pavement edge. All around him was pandemonium. He tried to lift himself up but found he could not move. It's like a bad dream, he thought, as his eyes saw the pool of blood swirl across the road. For a second Billy thought he could see his own reflection in the blood, then his vision went hazy.

Postscript

1977
Oliver's Army

The bright old day now dawns again; the cry runs through
the land,
In England there shall be dear bread - in Ireland, sword
and brand;
And poverty, and ignorance, shall swell the rich and
grand...

Charles Dickens (The Fine Old English Gentleman)

Neil McKinnon leaned back in his seat. It was dusk and the countryside flashed past the train window in a darkening blur. He pulled down the blind and rested his head back against the seat, but found he could not sleep. He had been thinking of his time in the army, and that last exercise in Kenya before he had managed, at last, to buy himself out.

He remembered Billy and the visits they had made to the 'local cafe'. He'd nearly missed the reports of Billy's death. When the first soldiers had been killed it had been headline news, but so many had died since then, and these days the army had difficulties recruiting, so now all a dead soldier warranted was a few lines on an inside page. By chance he'd come across a report in a paper at the bottom of page seven: it had started, 'Last night another soldier was shot dead in West Belfast...'

Neil thought of his visit to London and his mind filled with memories of the trip. He had been invited to speak at a Troops Out meeting in the capital, and had combined this with a visit to Wembley where he saw Scotland beat England 2-1. The Scottish crowd had seemed to outnumber the English at the match, and Neil had found himself behind a group of Scottish supporters, some wearing the red, white and blue of Rangers, and some the green and white of Celtic. They had all booed the English national anthem, drowning it out with the unofficial anthem of the Scottish fans:

> Oh Flower of Scotland,
> When will we see your like again,
> That fought and died for your wee bit hill and glen,
> And stood against him – proud Edward's army,
> And sent him homewards tae think again.

Neil's mind drifted to thoughts of the meeting. Nearly a thousand people had been crammed into a town hall. There had been a speaker from Belfast representing the republican movement, and Neil remembered the force of her commitment and the passion of her speech.

'I have not come to London to ask or beg support for the republicans in Ireland,' she had said. 'But I have come to to ask British people to look at, to find out, to understand what your forces and your politicians are doing in my country. And, based on that understanding, to ask British people to campaign for the withdrawal of your troops from Irish soil.

'I am always surprised that a country like Britain, which has many minorities within its borders, should take such a colonialist attitude towards a British minority in Ireland. But of course the British have one attitude towards their own people who went to other countries, and a different attitude towards the people of other countries who came to Britain to live.

'There are less than one million people of British descent in the North of Ireland, and there are over six million people of Irish descent in Britain. Suppose that I had come here tonight as a representative of those Irish people in this country. And suppose I were to tell you that we had a plan to move en masse to a specific area of England – let us say Manchester and the surrounding county. Then we all moved and became a majority in that area. And suppose we then said we were fed up with harassment under the so-called Prevention of Terrorism Act and the barrage of anti-Irish jokes, and we held a referendum. We, as the majority, then decided to secede from Britain and make our area – let us call it Middle England – part of Ireland, and we asked the Irish government to send troops and police across to uphold our law and order.

'And supposing some of the black minorities within your shores followed our example and did something similar. If that happened would Enoch Powell rush to support us? Would the establishment give us encouragement? Would politicians and political groups on the right, the centre and indeed the left, who construct grandiose theories to support the British right to do this in the North of Ireland, come and support us in this venture?

'When I first mentioned the idea I saw some of you smiling.' The republican woman slowly looked over the audience. 'Good, I would join you in that reaction – it is a ludicrous idea. No minority in this country would think of doing any such thing. But why are there still people of every political persuasion who insist on supporting people of British descent who do this in other countries?

'What then is the democratic, the socialist position towards an minority community inside your own country? Is it that they should not be discriminated against in any way? That they should have exactly the same rights as the rest of the population? I see many of you nodding your heads. I come to speak to you from a republican, socialist movement in Ireland which has exactly that position on the minority who regard themselves as British in our country. What we cannot grant them is the right to undemocratically keep our country divided any longer. We stand for a free united country, a secular country where no church can dominate, a socialist country where a united working class people will have control.'

When it came to Neil's turn he could feel the sweat trickling down. He always felt nervous speaking but persevered because of his commitment to securing the withdrawal of troops. He told the meeting about Britain's history of recent colonial small wars: Malaya, Cyprus, Kenya and Aden were some of the best-known examples. He said that most people in Britain were indifferent to what went on during those wars, because although British people gained at least some economic benefits through the continued exploitation that these wars were fought to safeguard, they did not want to hear the gruesome details of how those benefits were achieved.

He spoke of the tens of thousands of black Africans killed in Kenya in the fifties, and the hundred of thousands locked up in concentration camps. 'I feel shame when I tell you that Scottish soldiers were involved in this process. Scotland has a history of wars and men of war, but those famous names from the past like Wallace and Bruce fought for Scottish independence against English colonialism. Now Scotland's fighting men kill and harry peoples throughout the world at the command of the English establishment.'

It was his personal account of the anti–liberation war in Aden which made the biggest impact. Neil told his hushed audience about the man he and his unit had battered to death, just as he had told Billy in that tent in Kenya nearly ten years before. He recounted how the squaddies had been told that the Arab was a terrorist responsible for the deaths of other British soldiers. In reality, as Neil had found out afterwards, the murdered man had been a trade union organiser in the docks who, because of the level of repression against the local population by the soldiers, had organised a protest strike by dockers, who refused to unload British ships. That was why the Arab had become a target.

'The officers organised a contest between the units to see which could record the most kills. The unit next to ours had one more kill than us, and our officers and NCOs said we had to catch up. Each time a kill was made, the officers used to mark it up on the unit notice board. They did so by putting up one of these.' Neil held up a small flat object in his hand.

'And why did we kill him? Was it for democracy? Was it for people's rights? Was it to uphold the Queen's law and order?'

Neil looked at the audience and shook his head. 'No, it was for this.' He held out the object in his hand again. 'It's a golliwog, they give them away with jars of Robertson's jam. An officer had collected a box full and that's how they marked a kill.' Neil held up the golliwog. 'This is what we killed for, not for any lofty ideals, but because we wanted another one of these pinned up on our notice board.'

Neil's thoughts drifted back to the day Billy had been buried. The army had laid on a full military funeral with an honour guard and firing party from the regiment. Afterwards in a pub Neil had met a young soldier who was due to go back to the North of Ireland. The squaddie hadn't wanted to go back there, but he didn't want to desert either. So he was left with little choice. He complained that young soldiers like him were used as cannon fodder to keep the situation in check and preserve the status quo. A certain number of deaths and injuries were expected: as long as it could be kept to that 'acceptable level' the authorities were quite happy.

The young soldier had said that the only way to get a solution was to jerk the politicians out of their complacency. He had suggested that the next time an army unit was due to go to Belfast, a bunch of politicians should be sent in their place. 'Take a hundred Tories, a hundred Labour and a few of the rest and send them across instead. Give them SLRs and have them out patrolling the Falls. I bet there would be a political solution on the table quicker than you can say Jack Robinson.'

1980
The war continues

She has arisen –
From decades of humiliation,
From the pit dug by her enemy.

.

She arises.
When she arises
She will be fiercer than any beast,
And wiser than any man...

AI CH'ING

S orcha lay back in the bed and tried to ignore the plate of food on the table by the door. The women prisoners in Armagh were determined to carry out their hunger strike to the end if necessary, just like their comrades in the Kesh. Sorcha had been convicted in a Diplock court on the uncorroborated word of a man she had never seen before, but whose verbal evidence, delivered parrot-fashion, the judge had accepted. After serving six months of her fifteen-year sentence, Sorcha was elected OC by the women political prisoners, and had insisted on being the first one to go on the hunger strike

She tried not to think of the wasting process going on inside her own body, and to blot out such thoughts she let her mind drift into memories of the past. She remembered the visit she had made to London to speak at that Troops Out rally. It had seemed ironic to have been speaking on the same platform as the ex-British soldier. If he hadn't bought himself out they could have met on the streets of Belfast in different circumstances.

Sorcha's mind started to wander; it was the effects of her hunger strike, she told herself, as her thoughts flitted from one thing to another. She suddenly remembered the day about a week after Eileen's death when her friend's mother had brought around a box full of books. 'Eileen would have wanted you to have these,' she had said softly.

There was a half-finished article lying in the corner of the box. It was in Eileen's handwriting and was about the people of Ireland at the time of the first world war. Almost half a million Irish people had fought on Britain's side and almost a sixth of these did not return. The loyalists signed up and went on to make their blood sacrifice on the Somme because they were told it could help stop home rule. Three hundred thousand from the south also joined the British because they thought it would help bring home rule after the war had ended. George Gilmore, a republican and socialist, had told how he saw a recuitment poster in Belfast saying 'Fight Catholic Austria'. Taking it down he then went to Dublin and stuck it up again next to another recruitment poster which said 'Save Catholic Belgium'.

Most of Eileen's books were about the struggles of peoples in different parts of the world. As she read them Sorcha had seen that often the conflicts were so like their own fight in the North of Ireland. She remembered how Eileen had always argued that the republican movement should be building itself as a political organisation as well as a military one. Sorcha recalled the phrase Eileen had used: 'We don't want to find we have given so much to win the war, only to find we lose the peace.'

Sorcha laid her head back. She tired very easily these days, and could not concentrate for long. She smiled as she remembered the times when Eileen had given her lessons in her native language. There had been a book of Gaelic poetry and Sorcha had repeated the words after Eileen, who had then translated them. Remembering those poems, many of which dated from centuries ago, soothed her. She slowly spoke the words of the one that had been their favourite, written by an unknown seventeenth-century poet:

> May we not die, nor leave this valley of tears,
> Till we see the English go begging through the years,
> With packs on their backs to earn a paltry pay,
> In leaking old boots, as we did in our day.
>
> Time has conquered, and the wind scattered like dust,
> Alexander, Caesar; empires and cities are all lost;
> Tara is grass now, Troy flourished then fell;
> So even England – we may yet hear its death-knell.

Information on Ireland

Many people in Britain are deeply concerned about events in the North of Ireland but find it impossible to understand from national media coverage what is happening or why.

Information on Ireland is a voluntary group founded in 1978, which aims to provide information that is of concern to people in Britain but unavailable through the national media. The group is independent and non-profit-making. Since its formation in 1978, Information on Ireland has distributed more than 100,000 copies of its publications. Donations to help us with our work are very welcome.

BOOKS

Nothing But The Same Old Story: the roots of anti-Irish racism

An extensively illustrated and very readable account of the development of anti-Irish racism from the twelfth century onwards, showing how it has stemmed from England's colonial role in Ireland and how it is one aspect of the racism which Britain's rulers developed to justify their oppression of colonial subjects worldwide.

'I welcome this book and feel it will play a valuable part in helping to remove the negative and racist stereotyping which so often adversely affects the Irish community in Britain.' **Ken Livingstone**

Text by Liz Curtis
A5 size, 104 pages plus laminated card cover
Price (sterling) £2.50

The Irish Civil War 1922-1923 and what it still means for the Irish people

The civil war of 1922-1923 was a key event in Irish history which still influences Irish politicians, institutions and attitudes. Drawing on documents of the time, Frances M. Blake tells the story of the war and highlights the parallels with today.

In the mid-1970s, Frances M. Blake catalogued documents of the civil war period for the archives department of University College Dublin. After working on the papers of Republican officer Ernie O'Malley, she compiled and edited his best selling book on the civil war, *The Singing Flame*.

'A valuable education for those who would like to understand the conflict in Ireland.' **Brian MacDonald**, *Labour and Ireland*

A5 size, 72 pages plus laminated card cover
Price (sterling) £2

An Interlude With Seagulls: memories of a Long Kesh internee

Bobby Devlin was one of the thousands of people interned without trial in the North of Ireland in the early seventies. He spent two years in the grim 'cages' of Long Kesh prison camp. Here he tells mainly of the lighter side of internment. He recalls the comical incidents, the eccentric characters and the jokes, and some of the bad times too. His story reflects above all the spirit and good humour of his comrades that kept them going despite their difficult circumstances.

'Bobby Devlin skilfully blends a compilation of stories, many of which are now folklore, into an easy-to-read directory of resistance. The failure of the British to break the spirit of the internees is epitomised within the pages of **An Interlude With Seagulls**.' *Andersonstown News*

A5 size, 64 pages plus laminated card cover
Price (sterling) £1.50

Cormac Strikes Back: resistance cartoons from the North of Ireland

A selection of cartoons by Cormac, cartoonist for *An Phoblacht/Republican News* and some British socialist papers. Cormac's work gives a sharp, sometimes shocking and often very funny insight into the nationalist experience of British rule.

'It's bloody good strip cartooning, with a lot of parts that shock and a lot of parts that actually make you laugh out loud.' Steve Bell

A4 size, 96 pages plus laminated card cover
Price (sterling) £2.50

PAMPHLETS

They Shoot Children: the use of rubber and plastic bullets in the North of Ireland

A concise account of the history and use of these lethal weapons.

'A very powerful and timely pamphlet production. It documents, in a very effective and moving way, the history of the use of rubber and plastic bullets in Northern Ireland and further afield.'
Linton Kwesi Johnson, *Race Today*

Text by Liz Curtis
A5 size, 40 pages
Price 75p

A Resources Guide To The North Of Ireland

This guide lists a selection of books, papers, films, videos, organisations and other useful resources.

'The most comprehensive guide to where to find information on Northern Ireland. ...should be the starting point for anyone wanting to find out more about what is going on.'
Labour Research

A5 size, 32 pages
Price 50p

POSTER/MAGAZINE

The Case Of The Birmingham Six

An account of the wrongful conviction of the Birmingham Six, opening out into a dramatic black-and-yellow poster calling for them to be freed.

'It is a valuable piece of literature in the campaign to win justice for these unfortunate men. It provides a clear account of what happened to them and how they were unjustly convicted.'
Irish Post

A4 size, 4 pages plus A2 poster
Price 60p

Information on Ireland, PO Box 958, London W14 OJF.
Our publications are on sale in good bookshops or are available by post: just add 30p p&p per publication. Please make cheques/POs payable to Information on Ireland. Because of the high cost of changing foreign cheques, we can only accept payment in sterling. Or send a stamped addressed envelope for our leaflets.

Trade distribution:
Turnaround Distribution,
27 Horsell Road,
London N5 1XL.
Tel. 01-609 7836.

USA distribution by
Connolly Books,
PO Box 24744, Detroit,
Michigan 48224, USA.